KARI POHAR

Cassandra Seer

Psychic on the Run

First published by Wilson Lindberg Books 2026

First edition

ISBN: 979-8-9899469-6-9

Cover art by H M Lawson
Editing by Dennis Doty

This book was professionally typeset on Reedsy.
Find out more at reedsy.com

To Nick,
As long as we stick together, it doesn't matter who is on the wrong side of the river...we've got all the horses.

To Donna,
For believing in me so much that you read my vampire book.

To My Children,
May you always run toward your dreams, even when the wind is against you.

I'm eternally grateful to have you all in my life.

Contents

Easter Eggs

Each chapter title is an Easter Egg. They can reference: songs, TV shows, movies, and video games.

Can you find all the references?

Don't worry, if you can't. There's a guide at the back.

Kari

One

The Fool

"If I had never gone public with my abilities, none of this would have happened," I shouted into the phone. "If I'd kept it to myself, I wouldn't be a laughingstock."

Jack, my agent, sighed. "You're too sensitive. It's not that bad."

I groaned before asking, "How did the paparazzi find me at the beach, anyway? Have you heard where the leak came from?"

"It's been silent as a tomb." He laughed. "But maybe this isn't a *bad* thing. Look at it as an opportunity to tell your story. We can use this to bring your audience to your show. My phone has been blowing up with requests to have you on as a guest. Local news stations, podcasts, and talk shows all want to talk to you..." Jack droned on.

I let him drone on. The magazine that I had thrown to the floor a few minutes before caught my attention. The corner was bent from where it had landed. As I sat back up, I corrected my posture, something my mom found problematic.

The bold red title of the magazine read *Observer Weekly*. It was considered one of the trashiest tabloids on the market that was still in print. Their claim to fame was to tout bad photos of celebrities.

The October issue had a collage of celebrities as they enjoyed the last of the warmth. Many of them hit international beaches. Muffin tops, cellulite, dad bods, wrinkles, and a lone topless photo in the center. I had opted for a budget friendly beach that was in the next town over. That was the site where my first frontal nudity shot was taken. It was there for all the world to see. Two red fat arrows pointed at the imperfections on my body. This would be the public's first impression of me.

My brown eyes were wide with surprise as my brown hair flew around my head in tangles. The black and white polka dot bikini highlighted the deep red of my sunburnt shoulders. The bikini I chose that day wasn't the type of swimsuit I normally would've worn. I had been an expert at covering "problematic areas." In a moment of bravery, the week before, I bought the heavily discounted bikini.

The moment I had seen the black and white polka dots, it reminded me of the movie *Big Business* and the outfit Sadie wore. If Bette Midler could be a badass in polka dots, so could I. It did not wither away in my closet either. On the last warm day of the year, I put on the skimpy bikini and wore it to the beach.

It felt delightful to let go of the flowy swim tops. For a brief moment I hadn't cared if my body was a little jiggly. And cellulite be damned.

The thought of being a target for the paparazzi hadn't

crossed my mind. My show, *The Emberford Psychic,* hadn't aired yet. No one should have been there solely for celebrity photos. In my mind, I was a nobody.

Unfortunately, that was the day I realized my fame had caught up to me. It had become the worst beach day of my life. Not only did I have a killer sunburn, but a freak accident involving a dog, a seagull, and my bikini top gave the paparazzi everything they could have wanted in a photo. The blurb inside had added, "Cassandra Seer, from *The Emberford Psychic,* streaming soon on *Echo,* shows she couldn't predict that the sun would burn."

Jack interrupted my thoughts. "This could be the biggest break of your career. At least they blurred out your boobs. They would've had to put a cover to block it out otherwise. Probably could have charged more for that kind of exposure." His nasally laugh came over the line.

"I don't want my boobs for anyone to see," I snapped.

"I'll send over days and times to your personal assistant, Laverna. We're going to make sure you get a second season of *The Emberford Psychic.* If the first episode doesn't have a large number of views, they could cancel the whole thing before it's even given a chance. Your little 'snafu' is a blessing in disguise. It's perfect timing to get you in front of your target audience. Echo is releasing your first episode tonight. Appearing on these shows can help get people interested in your show. If you do these interviews, I can almost *guarantee* that you'll get a second season. The market hasn't had a new TV psychic for a while, so there isn't much competition right now," Jack rattled on. "You're going to be so busy!" I could almost hear the cha-ching as he calculated how much money he would be making off of my interviews.

We wrapped filming my debut show, *The Emberford Psychic, weeks ago.* As with other paranormal reality shows, the camera crew followed me around, and filmed me talking with residents, living and dead. Being a psychic was exhausting, because not only did I have to manage the barrage of chatter and demands from the spirits, but the living were equally as noisy and challenging.

The small town of Emberford had two stop lights, two grocery stores— the Mexican grocer, the chain supermarket, and a handful of cemeteries.

"I need a vacation," I murmured, unsure if the comment was addressed to Jack or myself.

"A vacation? I don't know about that..." he replied slowly. "Now's not the time to let go of the reins. Strike while the iron is hot."

"Yeah. I need to get out of here," I replied with more determination. I straightened my posture and continued, "I need to get away from everyone, the living and the dead."

"But..." Jack began.

I ignored him. "I don't want any interviews. Don't schedule them because I won't go. I'll be back sometime."

"If you don't do these interviews, my guarantee goes out the window. I can't promise that your show is going to be successful," he said. When I didn't relent, he shot back, "I've busted my ass to get you and this show on the air. It's the least you could do."

My heart pounded at the thought of going onto the bevy of shows. As I thought about it more, my arm pits began to sweat. "This is too much." Every negative thought I had been battling for the past few years spewed out of me, "Maybe it's better if I don't get another season. Maybe I'm not cut out for this business. Most people have normal jobs where they aren't followed around by a film crew. Nobody likes me anyway. Certainly not anyone in town. My own sisters barely tolerate me. My entire existence is me pretending to be above the harsh treatment I've received from everyone while no one gives me any kind of grace."

Before my show premiered, no one in town had a kind word to say about me or my family. We were all gifted in different areas in the psychic realm. My mother, Sybil, had a knack for knowing when someone was going to die. She hid it from most people and certainly didn't share that information with the producers of the show. On top of that, she was a gifted witch. Her host of spells and enchantments could help with most things a small town like Emberford could ever need. My dad, Rusty, was clairvoyant. He could always guess the number or color someone was thinking about, which was always a hit at parties.

Diana and Ilona, my sisters were twins and have mirror abilities. Diana had prophetic dreams, and Ilona had prophetic visions. When the incessant visits from ghosts from the cemetery across the street had gotten too much for them, they moved outside of the town limits. The spirits still asked me about them every single day.

At thirty-eight-years-old, I was recently single. Embarrassingly, I moved back in with my parents after a nasty break up with my ex-boyfriend, Zack. They were there to help pick up my broken pieces.

Zack and I had dated for a few years, and all I got out of it was crushing debt. I constantly paid both of our bills while he was chronically unemployed and self-indulgent in his whims.

A few years ago, when I had been approached by Jack to do

a reality TV show, Zack pushed me to do it. "This would really help us be able to keep our apartment, and your expensive car," he had said. So, I went forward with the deal with Jack in the hope that I would be able to keep up with Zack's spending.

I couldn't.

"We have to put up appearances that we have money. It'll attract more viewers. I'm doing this for you," he would tell me as he justified another purchase we couldn't afford.

The day my Toyota Corolla was repossessed, I parted ways with Zack. I thought the producers would be upset at the last-minute location change, but they were thrilled that my parents lived across the street from a cemetery. They attempted to get my parents involved in the show, but they both politely declined.

When I moved back into their home, the spirits from across the street must have missed me because they became an invasive species. My dad had gone so far as to put up a salt barrier that they could not cross. While they no longer could go into the house, they stood outside the salt line and called up to me. Their voices invaded my dreams. I had resorted to wearing earbuds and listening to music, but they still got through.

Despite the absence of the film crew, people in town suddenly found themselves interested in my family and made unannounced visits. We had yet to find a barrier they couldn't cross. To build a fence would take funds and labor that we didn't have yet.

If I could have gotten out of town and into a city, maybe I could've disappeared. The idea of being unrecognizable to people and spirits was intoxicating. It was worth a shot anyway. I had hustled hard to get my show picked up by a streaming service. With Zack no longer in the picture using up my money, my reason for doing the show seemed to be gone as well. My passion and drive had run dry. At that moment, I wasn't sure if it would ever come back.

Jack sighed heavily with frustration. "Fine. I can give you a max of a few days to rest. But after that, I need you back here, pronto."

"A few days? Pronto?" I asked, annoyed.

"I know. I know. I'm far too generous. Take a break and get back here," he complained. "Where are you going to go?"

Nervously, I laughed. "I don't know." When Jack started to say something, I interrupted. "And even if I did know, I wouldn't tell you where. I'll have Laverna inform you when I'm back in town. I shouldn't be gone more than a couple of weeks."

"A couple of weeks? That's not going to work for me. I can't have you gone that long…"

"It's not up for debate. Maybe take a vacation yourself!" I pressed the red button on my phone and disconnected the call.

Where was I going to go?

It didn't matter. Anywhere would be better than Emberford. In a flurry, I tossed in clothes, toothbrush, toothpaste, sunscreen, and anything else I could remember to grab and throw into the open suitcase. There would be plenty of places to purchase anything that was forgotten. Before I left, I grabbed a small blue plastic box by the handle and tossed it into the bag.

After the house was locked behind me, I jumped into my rusted 2009 black Mini Cooper and left town. The sun was still high, so I had plenty of time to figure out where I was headed before I needed to find a place to sleep.

I headed south toward the Indiana and Michigan border. Maybe I would go to Chicago and see the sights—The Bean, the museums, and theater.

As the distance grew between Emberford and me, familiar radio stations were replaced with static. I dug under my seat and found my trusty CD binder. In true Millennial fashion, I threw in a mixed CD that took me back to my youth. Green Day, Nirvana, Red Hot Chili Peppers, and Meatloaf, to name a few. My Mini was a base model and didn't come with Bluetooth so I had to use the methods of my youth to listen to my music.

As soon as my paychecks from *The Emberford Psychic* hit my bank account, I had paid off all of my debt. For the first time in years, my credit cards and car were paid off. I wasn't anxious to acquire anything I couldn't afford. My account sat at $4,354.88.

My parents didn't charge me rent and I continued to live frugally, probably due to the trauma of having a relationship with Zack.

After over two hours of driving toward the interstate, I stopped for gas and began to scour the internet for hotels that were in my price range. The ideal situation would have been to find one hotel I could land at for my entire trip. Someplace I could unpack and unwind without worrying about jumping from one hotel to another.

As I scrolled through the available hotels, I quickly realized that I would not be able to stay in Chicago. It simply would not be feasible for the amount of time I was hoping to be gone. The room alone for a few days would sap the amount I had decided I would be willing to spend on a hotel. It would leave nothing for dining or activities. I sighed heavily and said to myself, "Besides, I have no idea how long I'll be gone. I was hoping for a few weeks. I need somewhere much more budget friendly."

The further from the city that I zoomed out, the less appealing the attractions became. While the suburbs appeared nice in the stock photos, they weren't what I was searching for. I wanted night life and excitement.

A small, negative voice inside my head whispered, "Maybe you should go home and plan a vacation instead of leaving on a whim."

Desperate to not let the momentum die, I ventured further north on the map. Wisconsin! I had never been, but my appreciation for their cheese ran deep within me. While not the city-like adventure I had in my head, they too had some cities that might scratch the itch I was in search of.

"Once I get to the border, I'll find a rest area, and find some brochures of places to go," I said. Before my inner voice could say anything else, I threw the car into drive, and continued north to Beloit, Wisconsin.

When my stomach demanded to be fed a late lunch, I pulled into a fast-food drive through. I ordered some chicken nuggets, a side of fries, and a vanilla milkshake as a treat for myself. I had been through enough to necessitate a vanilla milkshake.

Before I left the parking lot, I ripped off the lid of the shake, dipped a few fries into the sweet treat, and ate them. Sure, most people wouldn't consider eating their French fries with their milkshakes, but it was my favorite type of dip.

The cupholders in the center console were filled with wrappers, Aldi quarters, lip balm, and a I love Jordan pin. I took the pin out and placed it into the glove compartment. It was kept in the car because it was a conversation starter.

"Who was Jordan?" I'd be asked. I would proudly tell them that Jordan Knight from the New Kids on the Block had been one of my favorites.

Seeing as how I was traveling alone, I didn't anticipate needing to start any conversations. The wrappers were tossed in the backseat. Something for future Cassandra to worry about and clean up.

When one of the drink holders was empty enough to hold the milkshake, I set it down. Inside the bag, I dumped the fries and nuggets into the bag and placed it between my thighs. It would be a surprise each time I reached in. Would it be a nugget or a fry?

Mindlessly, I ate while my brain was focused on following the directions on my phone. Woefully quick, my bag was empty, and it too was tossed into the backseat. With expert senses, I found the lid to the milkshake, slapped it on, and stabbed the straw through the hole. Since my favorite way to consume it was gone, I drank the rest the conventional way.

The hours clicked by on my dashboard clock and displayed 6:09 pm as I pulled into a rest area right off of I-39 in Wisconsin.

Luckily, it wasn't busy. I easily found a parking spot close to the surprisingly large building. The grounds were well maintained and landscaped. On either side were clusters of picnic tables. In the green space a pair of siblings ran around while a dog chased after them. Parents nearby watched and sighed heavily with relief. It looked like both the kids and dog were expelling their energy after hours in the car.

Inside, I used their facilities and wandered toward the large brochure rack filled with information on places to visit in Wisconsin. Travel magazines were stacked in a floor rack.

As I browsed through the brochures, they rustled slightly. Milwaukee and Madison stood out to me first, and I reached for some of their brochures. When I tried to pull one out, they were surprisingly stuck in place. I pulled harder only to rip one in half. As I gazed at the half in my hand, I said, "What is going on?"

With a tentative finger, I pushed the brochures aside to see what held them in place. When I saw no contraptions, I assumed it was some solidified sticky gunk at the bottom or back of the shelf that had cemented itself to the brochures.

Brochures for Door County would have interested me a few weeks ago, but I now had no interest in visiting any beaches for the foreseeable future.

I continued my perusing when the brochures rustled again. There was something weird going on, but I tried to ignore the impulse to search for a spirit. Who had ever heard of a rest stop that was haunted by a ghost? I shook my head and whispered, "It's probably the air conditioning. Or maybe someone had simply opened a door." Nonchalantly, I glanced around the entry but didn't see anyone.

With the need to find a place to go, I continued my search around the rack. Someone had not placed them in neatly and some were poking out a bit higher than others. The rustling continued. I grabbed the brochures at the top to stop them from moving. An icy chill ran through my fingers as I brushed against a spirit. Even at a rest stop I couldn't get away from ghosts.

Under my breath I released a series of expletives. "I'm on vacation," I hissed. "Leave me alone."

The spirit remained silent and invisible, but present. Most of the spirits that I came in contact with were at least partially visible and eager to talk. Whoever was in front of me did not provide a hint as to who they were. Tentatively, I reached a hand back out toward the spirit and felt a sharp icy smack as they hit my hand away from them.

"Fine. I'll leave you alone. You leave me alone too," I whispered. I refocused on the brochures and pulled some of them out. Oddly, the places like Cedarberg, Bayfield, and Milwaukee wouldn't release.

Without warning, a brochure flung up from the rack and hit me across the face. The edge scraped my cheek, and it stung immediately. That stupid spirit had given me a paper cut. While I held my fingers to my cut, I glared at the rack and hoped that it reached the spirit.

They remained hidden from me and didn't make a sound. "Just let me get my brochures and I'll be out of your way. Why on earth would you be so protective of this rack?" I hissed, but added, "Wait. I don't care. Just let go."

As I pulled on a random brochure, the spirit let go and I staggered back. I stumbled and almost fell. I shoved the brochure into my purse without looking down.

With a stamp of my foot, I shouted, "Dammit! I'm trying to go on vacation to get away from everyone. That includes everyone on either side of the spiritual plain."

Just then a woman and her gaggle of very small children followed behind her. She met my eyes and shot lasers at me through her glare, never losing eye contact. They hurried into the bathroom, away from me, an obviously disturbed woman.

As soon as they were out of sight, another brochure slipped up out of the rack and launched itself at my face. I blocked it with a smooth wax on, wax off move that Mr. Miyagi would have been proud of.

The rack began to shake violently. It looked like the spirit was going to push it over. Slowly, I backed away as the rack stopped shaking. A bunched bundle of brochures levitated and inched toward me. Only when I felt the glass of the windows behind me, did the brochures steadily gain on me. Whoever was advancing on me had a plan.

The bundle of brochures hovered in front of my face and shook slightly as if they were being held up by an invisible hand. A moment later, one brochure was tossed to the ground to reveal the one behind it. It only took three brochures for me to realize where the spirit was "encouraging" me to go. A touristy place called Wisconsin Dells.

"That's not what I had in mind," I snapped.

A brochure of a deer park floated closer, shook violently for a few moments before it flitted to the ground as it was tossed. The one behind that advertised something called a Duck tour. After the spirit shook it sufficiently, it tossed it away. A barrage of water park brochures, horseback riding, and horse drawn wagon rides were paraded in front of me.

"You're not going to leave me alone, are you?" I asked the empty space in front of me. I sensed that whoever was haunting me shook their head. A large bus of tourists entered the building, and I felt a hundred eyes on me. A few phones were held up. I could only imagine the videos they could capture and share. It could make me go viral for all the wrong reasons.

Under my breath, I hissed, "Fine, grab the brochures you want, discreetly. We're going to talk in my car."

A stack of brochures flew at my face, and I guessed that I was no longer going on a solo trip. I now had a passenger whether I liked it or not.

In my most stern voice, I said, "I need you to help me clean this up."

Between the two of us, we had all the brochures back in place, with a stack of possible places to visit in my bag in a few minutes. Just for fun, I grabbed a few brochures for Milwaukee and Madison, which now came free from the rack without a problem.

Two

One in a Million

Once I was back in my car, I heard the spirit sigh. He had followed me despite my desire for him to leave me alone.

After a slow, composing breath, I turned toward the spirit. "I did not invite you with me on this trip. Maybe you can find some other person to tag along with." The car rocked with their dissatisfaction at my suggestion.

The clock on the dashboard told me that I had wasted almost thirty minutes. It was going to be dark before I got anywhere.

"Why me?" I whined, but the spirit remained silent. With a frustrated grunt, I added sharply, "Fine. But if you're going to be on this road trip, I need to know your name. No more of this silent treatment. And don't throw things at me anymore. That is incredibly irritating."

A gruff man's voice bellowed, "I'm Bradley."

"More like Bratley," I snapped. "Why me?"

"Why not you? I've got places I want to see, and you've got a car. We're going to go on a road trip to a place I've always wanted to go back to," he said happily.

"I have not agreed to go to Wisconsin Dells," I complained, but I knew that I was going to take him there. I had a stage three clinger ghost, and I was afraid the only way to get rid of him was to take him there. Maybe I could drop him off and head somewhere that I truly wanted to visit after that.

With a quick search on my phone, I was pleasantly surprised to find several highly rated motels with reasonably priced rooms. For two whole weeks I could stay for under $1,000 and they included some free activities.

Even better, the place was only another hour and a half away. For a minute, I debated with myself about the pros and cons of the Dells or another place.

Pro: The place was in my budget.

Con: It was off season at the water park capital of the world. What else would even be open?

Pro: It was autumn and the leaves would probably be turning colors.

Con: But it wasn't Chicago.

With a resigned sigh, I booked a motel room for a night. If I could ditch Bradley somewhere, maybe I could find somewhere I would actually want to go. Quickly, I put the address into my phone, and we were off on my hijacked vacation.

He stayed silent as I drove. The night began to darken my path as the landscape became noticeably hillier. The silence drew wide between us, and my curiosity as to who my hitchhiking ghost grew.

"So, you happen to haunt a rest stop?" I asked.

"It's a long story," he replied shortly.

"And we got time. Another hour according to my GPS," I said with a wide smile. "Are you always invisible?"

He sighed heavily. "Yes. I'm always invisible. To tell you the truth, I don't want to get into it."

"If you need help finding your way to the light, I'm happy to guide you," I said hopefully.

"I didn't coerce you on this road trip to get me off this spinning rock. Silence is supposed to be golden. Maybe practice that instead of constantly chattering," he grumbled.

"You *are* a brat," I muttered under my breath.

"I heard that," he replied. "By the way, are you always this dirty?" In the rearview mirror, I could see empty fast-food bags, used napkins, and other odds and ends being tossed around the back seat. "Ew. There's so much garbage back here! You would think you would have learned how to clean up after yourself at your age."

With a sharp inhale, I gripped the steering wheel tighter.

To be fair, I hadn't expected company on my trip. If I had, I obviously would have cleaned up the car and displayed my New Kids on the Block pin to start a conversation.

For five minutes, I contemplated the benefit of going against my vow to only send spirits to the light when they asked. My mother's voice echoed in my head about what I put out into the world would come back to me three times. I had no interest in finding out what the consequences would be to send a spirit against their will. I still had no idea why he was drawn to Wisconsin Dells.

Instead, I stewed on imaginative ways to ditch him. The ones I was most proud of were (in no particular order):

1. Visit a war memorial and run away. Maybe he was a war vet or at the very least had a favorite war to learn about. He could easily be distracted so I could make my get away.
2. Finding another ghost in Wisconsin Dells to engage in conversation before running away while they were in deep discussion. Perhaps he would be more willing to chat with someone with a similar living status. While he was distracted I could drive away.
3. Making an "emergency" stop and asking him to get out of the car, then jump back in and drive away.
4. Abandon the car. It now belonged to him.

Under my breath, I grumbled, "Just so you know, I don't have money to get a room with two beds, much less a separate room for you."

Bradley sighed with exasperation. "You do know that I'm dead, right?"

"I had gathered as much," I replied. "I bet you were this delightful when you were alive."

"Of all people that I could catch a ride with, it had to be you. Don't make me regret my decision to ride with you," he replied.

I veered the car to the shoulder of the road and leaned over to open the passenger door. The wind caught the door as it swung open. "Don't let me force you on this trip. I encourage you to leave at any moment you like. Now, if it's convenient for you."

Something like a low growl escaped him and then went quiet. I imagined he was mentally making a list and contemplating the pros and cons of riding with me. Finally, he said, "No. I don't want to leave. Wisconsin Dells has always been on my bucket list."

The noise of the highway made it difficult to have a conversation, so I leaned back over but couldn't reach the door. I unbuckled my seatbelt and crawled over the passenger seat and yanked the door shut. "You're still working on your bucket list? I thought that was something you worked on *before* you died," I replied.

He sighed before he answered, "Typically, you work on it beforehand. But I figure, if I'm still haunting why not haunt in places that I've always wanted to see."

"So, you're hitchhiking to get to these places? Is that how you got to Beloit?" I asked. Secretly, I hoped he would give me more information about him.

Unfortunately, he only answered with a quick, "Yes."

When an idea crossed my mind, I changed topics and shot another question at him. "How'd you die?"

"That's not a pleasant topic for me," he answered.

"I'd imagine not, but I need some basic information about you before we get there," I demanded. "Otherwise, we're not continuing this little road trip."

"Fine," he grumbled. "I died at a forest preserve."

With a gasp, I asked, "Were you murdered? I figured forest preserves were decently safe."

"What kind of psychic are you? I thought psychics were supposed to be better at figuring out details of the deceased. Sounds to me like you're defective," he snarled at me.

"Typically, the ghosts or spirits are more helpful and *tell* me what happened to them. You are about as clear as a brick and just as dense," I snapped back at him. "And I will have you know that I am a very sought after psychic, especially by the dead. I have my own TV show. You would've heard about it if you weren't dead. You're the one that's defective, not me, mister."

With a huff, Bradley said, "I was hit by a tree branch."

I shifted uncomfortably in my seat and softly added, "That's horrible. I hope you didn't suffer. And I'm glad you weren't murdered. I'm not the type of psychic that helps with murder investigations. Blood makes me queasy."

"You are so strange," he said. For a moment I thought he dodged my questions again, but he added, "I was killed instantaneously. The worst part of it is that my doctor had recommended that I start walking for my health," he replied.

"Sounds to me like it was bad advice," I said.

"You can say that again. I haunted that doctor for a month entirely to get back at him," he growled.

Interest piqued, I leaned forward a little and asked, "Ooh. What did you do? Speak to him while he was asleep?"

"Mostly I moved things and put them where he wouldn't find them," he answered and asked, "You can talk to people while they're asleep?"

"Yeah, I think so. A few years ago, we had to put a protection around someone's house. That way uninvited spirits wouldn't get in. They would wander in during the night and influence the homeowners dreams," I disclosed.

He sniffed and replied, "Well, that's fascinating information to have."

"So, what did you do to the doctor?," I asked. "Did you throw a magazine at his face?"

"He couldn't hear or see me, and I wasn't skilled yet at getting someone's attention, like I am now," he chuckled.

"Sounds like something you could still use some work on. You've got the annoying part down, but the courtesy and communication are lacking," I added snidely.

Bradley sighed deeply. "I'm going to regret asking this, but you seemed nervous back there. Where were you headed before you ran into me?"

A lock of hair found its way between my fingers and I twisted it tightly. "Wisconsin," I said, finally.

"Wisconsin? But where in *Wisconsin?*" he asked.

With a shrug I said, "I'm on a last-minute road trip. There's no plan or agenda. I ride until something entices me to stop."

He sniffed sharply. "That's bullshit."

Instantly, I began to protest, but the lie felt exhausting to hold onto. "It is bullshit. I accidentally ended up topless on a tabloid cover, and now, I'm running away."

"You young people and your need to be naked. I simply don't understand it," he grumbled.

"I wasn't naked on purpose," I replied.

"How did you get naked by accident?"

"A seagull spotted me sunbathing at the beach and grabbed the strings on my bikini top. As I was trying to swat it away, a stray dog tried to grab the seagull mid-take off. Needless to say, my bikini top got away from me, and the paparazzi were waiting for me," I whispered. "Plus, I forgot sunscreen. I pulled the collar of my shirt back for him to see the burning red skin on my neck and back.

"That's certainly an adventure you've been on."

"Now, my blurred-out boobs are out there for the world to see. I needed to get out of town ASAP," I rambled.

"You young people aren't used to hard work and perseverance. Back in my day, stuff like this didn't happen," he said.

"How old are you? Cuz you sound about a hundred right now," I snapped. "Illegal and crazy stuff did happen back in 'your day,'" I continued. "I talk to ghosts and they're the biggest gossips. They spill the tea on *everything.*"

"That's insulting. I wasn't *that* old when I died." Stiffly, he added, "I was only sixty-five."

I nodded, "Well, that's not as old as you were acting. You must still be newly on the spirit side, because you're invisible."

"November seventeenth."

"So, you're getting close to your anniversary," I said softly.

He didn't respond immediately and when he did, he ignored my comment. "Can't say that I'm ever going to like you. You are far too chatty for my liking, but you're the first person in over a week that I've been able to get a ride with."

"Basically, beggars can't be choosers. But can't you hop in any car you want?" I asked. I had never thought about ghosts traveling before. Most of them had a radius or spot they stuck to. Bradley was the first hitch hiking ghost I had ever run across.

"You would think so, but haunting a car takes more finesse than I have. Just hopping into someone's car doesn't guarantee me a ride. Sometimes, I'll get in, but the car drives away without me. Other times, I go along for the ride. When you walked into that rest stop, you radiated light, and knew you were my ticket out of here," he said.

"I radiated light?"

A deep grumble escaped him. "Yes. Don't let it go to your head. It's strictly your aura and not your personality. Only a few people glimmer. They're the ones who have unwittingly given me a ride."

I ignored the jab and instead asked, "Do you know why some people glimmer?" No ghost had ever talked about glimmers or radiating light to me. I wondered why this was the first time I was hearing about it.

"The only thing I know is that the glimmering ones seem a bit more…sensitive. A bit too touchy," he replied with judgment dripping from his tone.

"So, you're going to insult the people that helped you get around. That's really considerate of you."

"See? Touchy," he snapped. When I only glared at him, he finally added, "If it would make you feel better, I'll try to be less *judgmental.*"

"Thank you," I said. "Wisconsin Dells, huh?" I asked.

"I always wanted to go back. My parents used to take me when I was a kid," he replied.

Around us, the sky had darkened and the need to get back on the road called me. Without another word, I turned my turn signal on and merged back onto the road. We were both silent the rest of the way to Wisconsin Dells.

***

It was dark as we got closer to our stop. Large waterpark hotels with brightly colored water slides that wrapped around the building surrounded chain restaurants and shopping areas.

"Corporations see a pristine place like this and instantly know they can improve it. They can't leave gems like this alone, can they?" Bradley huffed.

"We still have a way to go to get to our place. This seems entertaining though. There's something for everyone here," I replied brightly. "Imagine all the fun families have with their kids. Admit it, you would have loved to stay at one of these hotels as a kid.

Under his breath, he sneered, "Destroy my childhood why don't they."

With a shrug, I drove on. Slowly, the large hotels disappeared behind us, and smaller hotels and motels loomed ahead.

"This is what I remembered!" Bradley shouted with joy in his voice. "These small motels. My parents always made sure we stayed somewhere that had a pool." He grew silent and I knew he was reminiscing on the days that had passed him by.

Through a bustling downtown area with more restaurants, attractions, and shops, we finally could see our destination on my phone's map. We turned the corner and saw a motel that appeared that the owners hadn't updated the place since the 1960's. Parking, astroturf, and webbed patio chairs were outside each room.

Instead of being out of style, it gave vintage vibes. It felt like something that had lasted time and reminded me of a bygone era. Certainly, for those seeking modern facades and large water parks, this type of accommodation wouldn't be attractive to that clientele. For someone who wanted a sense of being secluded from the rest of town, this would be perfect.

The lobby was a separate building in the center of a horseshoe of rooms. Behind the lobby was another building that I assumed was an indoor pool. An updated playground and picnic tables provided space for parents to allow their children to expend some of their energy.

As soon as I parked my car, I knew I needed to make a decision on whether to stay or go. For a relatively inexpensive motel, at first glance it seemed ship-shaped and clean. Honestly, the motel offered everything that I needed for a reasonable rate.

Once in the office, I checked in and asked to add on additional days. They gladly charged my card for the additional days. With the key in hand, I drove my car behind the pool building and parked at my door. When I opened it, the coldness of the room blasted me in the face.

Where the outside was a blast from the past, the inside provided a more modern take on mid-century motel. The bedding had a maroon and gold design, typical of most midwestern motels. New floors had been installed recently along with fresh paint on the walls.

I tossed the bags I carried on the floor and jumped onto the bed. Silence was the only thing that I heard. As far as I could tell, the only spirit at the motel was the one that I brought with me. Hopefully, it would stay that way.

"Well, Bradley, we need to have an understanding of boundaries," I said as I slid off the bed and turned around the room. He wasn't making noise, and I couldn't tell where he was standing. After he grumbled, I continued, "When I'm in the bathroom, you are not allowed to peek in."

"What kind of person do you think I am?" he asked. "I'm not a pervert."

"Imagine I was your daughter. What would you want her to say to some random guy she picked up at a random rest stop in Beloit, Wisconsin?"

"Understood," he replied quickly.

"I saw a fast-food restaurant down the street and a gas station nearby. I'm going to grab myself something to eat and pick up a few things for tomorrow," I said.

"Why go to a convenience store when you would get better prices at an actual grocery store? Your generation is all about convenience and not enough about saving money. You all complain you can't afford anything," he declared.

After a deep, calming breath, I reminded him, "Please remember, I did allow you to come along on a trip to the place *you* wanted to go. Insult me one more time and I may send you to the light when you're least expecting it."

He sighed heavily and asked, "Is that even something you can do?"

With hands on my hips I answered, "Yes, I can. It's exhausting, but I have a whole motel room that I can recover in if I need to send you."

"At least take your pepper spray. Never know when someone could attack you," he replied.

I shook my head as I grabbed my purse to head down the street. It made sense for me to walk, rather than drive. It wasn't going to be far.

After only a minute or so, I heard Bradley next to me. "Shouldn't you have your pepper spray out?"

Without acknowledging his comment, I pulled my sweatshirt tighter around me as I made my way to the restaurant. It was chillier than I had expected.

"Of course, you don't have pepper spray," he said.

"I thought this place was 'family friendly.' Why would I need pepper spray here?," I asked.

He only grumbled in response.

As we crossed the street and walked past the gas station convenience store, I said, "You don't need to be here. Go back to the motel. Or does the idea of being away from me cause you distress?"

"Ha! You wish. It's more like I'm trying to keep you alive," he replied.

"I've been an adult for…" I began and counted out how many years I had been an adult but didn't like the number I came up with. "A long time."

He made a soft humph sound. "I want to test how far away I can get from you before I have difficulty moving to other locations. Based on how strong your aura is, I'm hoping to be able to see everything in the Dells without you."

"So, if I leave, you could be stuck here?" I asked.

"That's my fear. This is only the first place on my list, and it's taken me this long to get here," he replied.

At the restaurant, I ordered a cheeseburger, fries, drink, and paid almost fifteen dollars. The expensive upgrade for a fancy milkshake with a donut stuck on top was out of the question. I would have to eat my French fries the boring way. But it would have helped make up for the fact that I now had a ghost tagging along with me.

While the convenience store would be more expensive than a grocery store, it would be better than take-out every day. I couldn't imagine how much I would spend on food alone on the trip.

When I'd eaten and taken my tray to the garbage, I began the hike back to the store. After only a few minutes, my throat felt on fire. Heartburn, thanks to having fast food twice in one day. In college, I'd been able to eat as much as I wanted without any ill effects. Now, however, heartburn could attack at any moment. I'd have to grab some anti-acids as well.

Inside the convenience store, it was warm and bright. The cashier glanced up from the magazine she was reading and smiled faintly. "Welcome!" As soon as I moved further into the store, she put her face back into her magazine.

That's when I noticed the name of the magazine. *Observer Weekly*. Panic shot through me at the thought of being recognized. I ducked behind some shelves and quickly searched for items. The sooner I got out of there, the better.

It was a well-stocked store, and I was able to find some staple food items—applesauce, a few microwave pasta bowls, a bag of off brand cookies, and a couple of premade ham sandwiches. I would get to an actual store soon, but for now, these would get me by.

When I had everything, I placed my items on the counter, and the cashier put her magazine down. "Good evening! Did you find everything you needed?" she asked as she began to ring up my purchases.

"Y...yes," I stammered.

She took her time and carefully bagged each item. "You seem familiar. Do you live around here?" she asked.

Vigorously, I shook my head. "Nope. First time here. I must have one of those faces, ya know?" I shrugged.

"Your total is $45.97. Can I interest you in our king-size candy bars? They're on special today."

"No. Thank you," I replied and tapped my credit card on the machine.

She held my receipt out to me but kept a hold of it as she examined me closely. In real time I watched as recognition washed over her face. "I know who you are!"

I snatched the receipt and ran out of the store. The moment I was outside, the wind and cold hit me in the face. I crossed the street and increased my pace to go back to the motel. Luckily, it only took me a few minutes to get back, and I could see the lights from the parking lot in the distance. The bag in my hand felt heavy and I hoped that it wouldn't break on the way.

It lasted until the moment I opened my motel room door. Then it ripped and spilled the contents on the ground.

With a sigh, I picked up the food and juggled the applesauce container with my feet to get into the room.

Once all the food was put away, I tackled my suitcases. My clothes were put away in the drawers, while hygiene items were placed in the drawers in the sink outside the bathroom.

After a quick shower, my bed beckoned me.

"I'm going to bed, Bradley," I announced, unsure if he was even in the room with me. I stood silently for a few moments before saying, "Night. Talk to you in the morning."

Three

The Peanut Butter Solution

A barrage of chirps from my phone woke me up before the sun was up. The "Do Not Disturb" feature on the phone had turned off. With blurry eyes, I attempted to focus on the screen and watched in real time as hundreds of texts flooded my phone. On top of that, there were several missed phone calls with matching voicemails from my mother. I didn't bother listening to the voicemails.

Mom: Where are you? You didn't come home last night... Do I need to file a missing person's report?

Dad: Hey there, firecracker! Thought we were going to watch your show with you last night? Everything alright?

Mom: Cassandra Sorcha Seer. You respond to me right now. You have me worried. Where are you?

Dad: Earth to Cassandra. Where have you wandered off to?

Mom: Text or call me to let me know you're ok.

Ilona: Cass, where are you? Mom is freaked out. Please don't end up dead in a ditch. I don't have time to help with your funeral right now.

Diana: If mom dies from heart failure, I'm blaming you.

Mom: I know you're not dead, but there are things that can happen to women that are far worse than death. You need to tell me where you're at. Now.

Jack: Cassie, baby! Your show was a massive hit (thanks to this guy!). Let's chat! Call me!

Jack: We need to chat about promoting your show. TV spots, local news stations, podcasts. The sky's the limit!

Jack: Cassie. You need to get back here. We have to strike while the iron is hot!"

Jack had sent almost twenty texts throughout the night. While I was thankful I had slept through them, I could not reply to a single one without my heart hammering in my chest. Instead, I scanned each message but did not respond. Unfortunately, he would see in his messages that I had seen them.

Other texts were from family friends and acquaintances who had sent me congratulations on the success of the first episode of my show. In my rush to get out of Emberford, I had forgotten it aired last night.

I groaned as I rolled onto my back. "I wish I could create a reply to one person and send it out to every single person." Instead, I did not open those texts. They didn't deserve to know I had read their message and didn't respond. My parents and sisters needed to know I was safe, though.

In the family group chat, I texted simply: Sorry, all! I needed to get away. Everything got to be too much. I'm safe and taking a much-needed break from life. I'm planning on being in the Dells for a while. When I'm ready to face reality, I'll come home."

> *Dad: About time you let us know where you were. Mom was about to drive around until she found you. Even without a location, she would have scented you out like a bloodhound. She didn't sleep all night. I'm going to get her to take a nap.*

> *Ilona: Glad you're not dead. I didn't think you were but thank you for the confirmation.*

> *Diana: You should know that this stunt took off a few years from mom's life. I would never have done that to her. That's why I'm her favorite.*

My mother responded with a call instead of a text.

The moment I pressed answer, she began to talk and didn't bother waiting for a hello. "You may be an adult, and you may have forgotten the rules of our household. If you're not going to be home overnight, you let someone know. No one knew where you were." Her normally soft mid-Western accent was harsher than I had heard it since I was a teenager.

"Sorry, mom," I replied sheepishly.

With a deep sigh, she said, "So you're escaping? It's not always wise to hide away from your troubles."

"I know, but it's more of a vacation. Good escapism, right? I've worked so hard that I think I deserve a break," I said. "Sounds like my show was a hit."

"You should see it. It highlights and shows everyone what we've known all along." Softly, she added, "Your talents and gifts are in the way you connect with people, the living and the dead." When I didn't say anything, she continued, "If I ever get my hands on the person that took those photos of you, I'll let them know when they're going to die. But, until then, can you *please* tell us when you're taking off? A simple hand-written note on the fridge would have sufficed."

I nodded and agreed, "Yes, Mom."

"Take whatever time you need. Your father and I are here, should you need us," she whispered.

Tears sprang to my eyes and we said good-bye. Then the reality of the past few days came into focus. My throat felt like it would close on me at any moment. The embarrassment of being naked on the cover of a tabloid, being stalked by the paparazzi, Jack's pressure to be on a variety of shows, and finally, picking up the world's most stubborn spirit I had ever had the displeasure of meeting felt like too much. The weight of everything felt heavy on my shoulders. Now, I was on a vacation that I wanted but knew Wisconsin Dells was not where I wanted to be.

The disappointment of not being able to afford Chicago was weighing on me. Anger bubbled under the surface as my mind focused on not being able to choose where I went on vacation. All of my frustrations landed squarely on Bradley, regardless if they were all his. I didn't want more contact with Jack, since I had successfully gotten away from him. But I found myself being controlled by another man. Would I ever have control over myself, and what I wanted?

"Why am I here?" I whined.

From the corner of the room, Bradley asked, "You doing ok, Cassie?"

I threw the blanket off of me and jumped out of bed. With a fury I rarely felt, I stormed to the corner where I suspected he was. "You took over this vacation for me. This was supposed to be my escape from life. Now I'm up in some motel in the middle of nowhere. You didn't care if this was where I wanted to go. All that mattered was your stupid bucket list," I yelled.

He grumbled before saying, "I'm going for a walk. Emotional women are too much for me."

"Like hell you are! You're the reason I'm emotional," I shouted. My light jacket hung near the door, and I grabbed it as I ran out the door after him. With my breath heaving as I raced after him, I hissed, "Chasing you down would be a whole lot easier if you weren't invisible."

Ahead of me, I could hear him as he grumbled. Gravel crunched under my feet as I hiked down the drive and onto the side of the road. Bradley had gone annoyingly quiet. I scanned to see if I could get a clue as to which way he had gone.

On the blacktop, a large black cat with wide green eyes sprawled out, soaking up the sunlight. Without warning, it jumped up, ears pulled back as it made a series of hisses and spits at something I couldn't see. With an arched back, its sleek tail grew three times larger.

Then I heard Bradley hiss back at the cat and I knew which direction he had gone.

I sped up my pace to catch up to him, but the moment my feet touched the blacktop, I staggered. The sensation was akin to a thread being pulled from me. A prickling from somewhere behind my belly button startled me.

Something or someone wanted me to turn left. Despite my best efforts to turn right, my feet led me to the left.

"Here's another thing I can't even decide myself!" I shouted. My feet may have known the direction, but I made sure to stomp my feet to get out the anger and frustration that coursed through my body. There was no way for me to know how far the destination would be. With a pat on my pocket, I ensured my phone was safely tucked inside in the event I needed to call for help.

Less than a half mile later, without warning, it released and I found myself standing across the street from a cemetery. The front of the grounds was lined with a white wooden fence. The entrance, however, was far grander.

The black iron gate was shut and locked. Willow Crest Cemetery was written in thin white letters across it. On either side of the gate was a long curved white concrete fence, which was tinged green from the trees. No one had cleaned it for a long time.

"I wouldn't get closer," Bradley called from across the street. "I don't think this place is for you."

"Now you're trying to tell me where I can and cannot go?" I yelled.

"I just need a moment," he said.

"Oh! Do my big woman emotions make you uncomfortable?" I shouted.

"They do. Go back to the motel."

"Don't tell me what to do!" I shouted. "Every man in my life, except for my dad, tells me what to do. I'm a grown ass woman and can make my own decisions."

"You wanted to stand across the street from an old cemetery?" he said caustically.

I sighed. "No."

"Go back," he said.

Before I could reply, my feet moved again on their own. Slowly, I walked across the street.

"I already told you!" I snapped. "However, I don't seem to have control over this…" My words trailed off as I began to sense the spirits within the cemetery. I groaned inwardly at being spotted, anticipated at being mobbed by a bunch of ghosts.

But they didn't move toward me. Instead, they all seemed sleepy and sluggish. It was almost like they didn't even notice my presence. Without thought, I took another step closer to the cemetery, my arm lifted to reach for the spirits.

A chill burned through my hand and I stopped midstep. "Cassie, go back to the motel and get some more sleep. We've got a full day of fun things to do later," Bradley whispered in my ear. Slowly, I realized that Bradley had grabbed my hand and I had control again over my body.

I shook my head. "Why would I want to do anything with you? You don't talk to me and make every single conversation difficult. This is on your bucket list, not mine." I spun on my heel and began to walk away. When he didn't respond, I yelled over my shoulder, "And don't call me Cassie!"

I stomped back to the motel and stewed in my fumes. In my rage, I downed a few cereal bars and a box of raisins from my small stash of food I had packed from home. The rest of my food called to me, and I wanted to eat it all, in the hopes of drowning my anger. Instead, I decided to walk around the almost empty parking lot.

Under my breath, I grumbled, "I'm doing this for my stupid mental health."

Being a Monday in October seemed to mean that fewer people stayed at the motel. Before I retreated back to my room, I stopped by the pool and hot tub area to check it out.

There was no one inside and I stuck my hand into the water. It was warmer than I expected. There was a slide that ended in the three-foot area of the pool. With new trauma surrounding swimwear, I had opted to bring a different style with me. Any bikini would forever be banished. Again, I wished I had decided to stay home that day and enjoy the last warm day of the year reading on our porch. If I had, I never would have ended up on the cover of that magazine.

I shook my head in a feeble attempt to get the picture of the photos out of my head. When that didn't work, I went back to my room with the hopes of getting my swimsuit on to go for a swim. As soon as I got back into the room, I laid on my bed to stretch out a few moments. But that moment turned into a few hours.

When I opened my eyes again, I felt groggy.

"Good evening, princess," Bradley growled. "Sleeping the day away, I see."

With a heavy sigh, I pushed myself to sit up. "I'm on *vacation*. Why does it bother you if I take a nap? Obviously, if I fell asleep, my body needed some rest."

"Your generation…" he began, but I interrupted him.

"I know. I know. My generation is a bunch of lazy, worthless babies. We're too sensitive. Too politically correct. Can't take a joke," I snapped.

"I *never* said that," he hissed.

"You might as well have. I can't be in this room with you anymore. It's like you suck the life out of everything. Probably because you're dead," I snapped. "I'm going to the pool." I got up and retrieved my swimsuit from a drawer.

"Is that the wisest decision? You know what happened last time?"

"Gah!" I yelled with my swimsuit in hand. Near me was the thermostat and I turned it up to warm the room.

I stomped to the bathroom to get changed. For the rest of the evening, I swam laps in the pool and tried to ease the anger Bradley brought out in me. After fifteen rage fueled laps, I was exhausted and eased myself into the hot tub to relax for a few minutes.

The only problem with the hot tub was how cold it made the walk from the pool house to my room. With a few towels bundled around me, I scurried across the parking lot and fumbled with my key to open the door. Finally, I got the door open, only for a blast of chilly air to hit me.

Hurriedly, I raced into the room to switch the heat back on. "I'm sure I turned on the heat and not the air conditioner," I said to myself.

Bradley's chuckle came from the corner. "Sorry. I couldn't help myself."

"Ahh!" I shouted, pulled out a pair of pajamas from the drawer and stormed into the bathroom. "You better watch it. I'll drop you off in the middle of nowhere and leave you there."

"I'm going to haunt you until the day you die," he snarled.

I slammed the bathroom door behind me and got into the

shower. I let the hot water steam up the room before I even began to wash the chlorine off of me.

By the time I left the bathroom, my rage was duller. Daydreams of where I could leave Bradley brought a smile to my face.

From the mini-fridge, I grabbed a sandwich and the jar of applesauce. I didn't have any bowls, so I grabbed a spoon from a packet of utensils and ate from the jar.

For the remainder of the evening, I flipped through channels on the TV and was pleasantly surprised at the number of offerings the motel offered. In the past when I stayed at a hotel, there were few choices available.

It was early when I shut off the TV and lay down to go to sleep, but sleep was elusive. For a few hours, I listened to random podcasts and played games on my phone. Then finally, sleep found me.

In the early hours of the morning, my body shivered uncontrollably. Without opening my eyes, I reached my hand out to search for the blanket, but it was not on me. When I opened my eyes, the blanket and sheets were piled on the floor.

Quickly, I jumped out of bed and blinked to get my eyes to adjust. As I staggered to the thermometer, I tripped over the blanket pile and nearly fell to the floor. When I brought my face closer to the dial, I saw Bradley had turned the air conditioner onto full blast.

I shouted obscenities to the room as I turned the heat back up. If Bradley was still in the room, he didn't give away his location. I doubted he stuck around because I was sure he wouldn't have been able to keep himself from laughing at his trick.

I threw the blankets back onto the bed and grabbed the jar

of applesauce and a spoon before getting under the blankets. When I found a Lord of the Rings marathon on TV, it made my decision to bed rot easy. I would not be leaving the room for the entire day.

My grudge I held against Bradley wasn't helped by his antics. He wasn't grateful and had yet to thank me for bringing him on the trip with me. I knew I was pouting. No one back home would have allowed me to wallow in my misery. My mother would have made me garden with her. Dad would have rattled on about something that had happened to him when he was a kid. Ilona and Diana would have bragged about their spirit-free home but not invite me to stay with them. They would have made me beg to sleep over for a few nights.

Here, I could embrace my misery. I could stew in my anger and focus it all onto Bradley. It seemed that he was equally as mad as I was. He didn't make his presence known to me that entire day. Before bed, I realized I had eaten all of my food.

I would have to go to the store the next morning first thing. There was no way for me to put off a shopping trip any longer. So, as the sun began to rise on Wednesday morning, I was dressed, address of a local grocery store in my map app, while my stomach roared at me.

As I began to check into the prices, I quickly decided that sandwiches and chips would be the cheapest option for my current situation, since the motel did not provide any meals. After peanut butter, jelly, a container of lunchmeat, cheese slices, and various snacks were placed in my cart, I approached the registers.

A small line filed to the lone cashier in a pair of khaki pants and a dark green polo with the store's logo printed on the right side. As I waited, *The Observer Weekly stared* at me and my eyes would not leave the blurred spots where my boobs were. My sunglasses were in the car so there was no hope for me to hide my identity further. I hoped no one would notice me.

Thankfully, the short cashier was speedy. She smiled politely to the customers but didn't chat. Her name tag read, "Alice." Her light brown hair was tied back, and it rested over her left shoulder.

Soon, she began to scan my items but didn't peek up to greet me. I found a piece of broken tile under my foot and dropped my head to feign interest in it to keep my identity hidden.

That's when I heard something shatter as it hit the ground. My head snapped up and saw Alice's mouth fall open. She whispered, "You're the *Emberford Psychic*." At her feet lay the glass jar of grape jelly. Shards of glass scattered across the white linoleum flooring. Purple jelly oozed from what remained of the jar at her feet.

"Shh," I whispered and shook my head.

The light flashed at her numbered kiosk and quickly a manager jumped onto another lane to check out the people who had lined up behind me. Another employee was asked to bring up cleaning supplies and an announcement over the intercom asked for a replacement jar of the jelly.

Alice replied in a soft voice, "I'm so sorry."

"It's ok. It was an accident," I replied.

Suddenly, she blurted, "I saw your show. It was mind-blowing."

My face fell, and I glanced around me. Who all had heard her? Was she going to tell anyone I was here? What was I going to do if they found me?

Hurriedly, she asked. "Is everything you do in your show real?"

I nodded slightly. "I need to get going. Can we finish?"

Alice tucked a loose lock of hair behind her ear, "I hoped you were a *real* psychic. How long are you going to be in town?" My groceries were forgotten on the conveyor belt.

"A while, I guess. As long as the paparazzi don't catch wind of where I'm at," I said softly. "I do need to get going."

She crossed her heart with her forefinger. "They won't hear it from me." Alice scanned my last few items and bagged them.

"I appreciate that."

From behind Alice, another worker handed her an identical jar of jelly. She added it to my purchases in one of the bags and I paid. With my purchases in hand, I fled the store.

The moment I stepped into my room, Bradley stated, "It's about time you bought yourself some real food from a real store. Seems like you're done with your temper tantrum now."

"My temper tantrum? Seems to me you've been the one acting out like a moody teenager," I snapped back. "By the way, hello to you too."

"See you've still got your spicy pants on."

"I don't see you apologizing or even thanking me for bringing you on this little trip," I retorted. When he didn't reply, I hissed, "What am I even doing here? I wanted a bustling city, not some off-season tourist trap."

"Seems to me you needed some quiet over a busy city," he said, the gruffness eased from his tone. "What have you explored since you got here?"

I hesitated before saying, "The grocery store and the road to the cemetery."

He grumbled as he moved closer to me. "Go explore this morning. Things will start opening up soon then you'll see how alive this place can be."

"You didn't want me anywhere near that cemetery. Should I go there?" I asked sharply.

"There's something not right about that place. I don't like it there and don't plan to go back. I can only imagine what they would want with a psychic there," he replied.

"It is weird there and I wasn't planning on making any more trips there, thank you very much."

"Good. But you should get out of the room. It'd be a shame for you to leave now and not experience what the Dells can offer," he added softly. "Besides, if you stay, I can explore more. I've been able to wander all over while you sleep."

"So, this doesn't have anything to do with my happiness. It's all about what you want, huh? You don't want me to abandon you here," I snapped.

"I think you'd be surprised at what you may enjoy here."

"Why do you care if I just stay in the room? Staying in is safer for me," I replied.

"Safer? Sure. But what will you remember from this trip? Nothing. And then before you know it, it'll be on *your* bucket list and have to come back. Get out of this room. Go talk to people. Go eat at some local restaurants. If you were in Chicago, would you be rotting away in bed all day?"

My head hung when I replied, "No."

"If you waste this time it won't be my fault. It's going to be yours for not getting out there to see what you can do."

Frustrated, I grumbled, "Are you tagging along?"

"Nope. I've imposed my desire to be here on you long enough. It's not working anyway. You're insufferable. Doesn't seem right to force you to do everything I want. Go out and see what pulls your interest," he encouraged. A tingling traveled up and down my back, and I realized he had touched me.

I sighed and released some of my frustration. According to my sister, Diana, that was how wrinkles and premature aging occurred.

"It's taken me to become a spirit to start to understand that time doesn't move at the same speed. It's slower on this side. I guess when you take the urgency out of your existence what else do you have but time? Don't waste your time here. There's more to life out there than fear."

I nodded and grabbed a paper map of the town with attractions listed with numbers and headed to explore whatever the Dells had to offer.

Four

Extensive Collection of Name Tags & Hair Nets

The bustling downtown area caught my attention, and I found a parking lot. The shops and businesses were open, and people buzzed around with their purchases. The smell of local food wafted in the air and beckoned me to try some of the local cuisine.

As with any tourist location, some of the shops hawked marked up cheaply made souvenirs. I learned fairly quickly which shops to avoid after I wandered into a few of them.

However, it was the unique shops that drew me to them. A gaming store, a rock shop, a sword shop, and others which were busy with foot traffic entering and leaving their stores.

With an eye keenly on my spending, I purchased a small, shiny tiger's eye and a pretty bracelet for my mother.

The attractions were sprinkled amongst the shops. A video arcade, a boat tour, a mirror maze, an escape room, and a giant place that touted a live-action fantasy adventure.

While I wore my pair of black sunglasses, I felt like I was incognito. No one stopped me or even glanced my way. Either my disguise was effective or else Wisconsin wasn't the target audience for the *Emberford Psychic*.

Autumn had arrived in the Dells, and everyone wore sweatshirts and jackets. The sun shining overhead was deceiving as the air had autumn crispness.

As I took in the sights, sounds, and smells of the area, someone from behind me tapped me on the shoulder. Startled, I jumped and spun around. Alice, the cashier from the grocery store, smiled at me. She was still wearing her work uniform, complete with her name tag.

Slowly, I said, "Hey, Alice."

She blushed and fidgeted with her fingers, "You remembered my name."

I pointed to her name tag, "I do, but you're still wearing your name tag."

Quickly, she unclipped the pin from her shirt and shoved it into her purse. "Sorry to bother you. I was walking by and saw you," she said then dropped her head in her hands. "That sounds like I'm stalking you."

I smiled. "Go on. I don't get stalker vibes off of you."

Her mouth opened and asked, "You can tell if someone's a stalker?"

With a laugh, I shook my head. "No. That's not the vibe I get from you."

"What vibe do you get from me?" she asked instantly. Then a blush crossed her cheeks. "Sorry. You don't have the answer there. I wanted to apologize to you at the grocery store, but you rushed off. It feels a bit like kismet to run into you here. I needed to pick up something for my mom on my way home and just happened to see you standing here. I'm sorry for taking up your time at the store...and also for taking up more of your time here."

Sincerity poured off Alice like water.

With a soft smile, I said, "That's ok. Who hasn't dropped a glass jar and broken it? I once dropped a giant jar of salsa from Costco. We were cleaning up salsa for hours."

She laughed. "Well, thank you for that."

"Are you off for the rest of the day?" I asked.

"Yeah. And the rest of the week," she said and then added, "Possibly forever. They told me I broke too many things and are reconsidering my employment."

"I'm so sorry, Alice. Is there anything I can do?" I asked before I could stop myself.

"Oh, no. I'm ok. My dad says I need to learn how to manage my anxiety when I'm at work."

"I have found that if it's the right employment, the anxiety lessens. Maybe you need to find a different type of work," I suggested.

She laughed half-heartedly. "Every job I've had makes me nervous. In the customer industry, they typically don't seek people who are nervous. I don't enjoy being yelled at by customers. Or bosses."

I patted her shoulder awkwardly. "Nobody wants that."

Alice shifted her purse and asked, "What are you doing today?"

With a shrug I replied, "No idea. My g...friend. My friend sent me off with this map to go explore this place with." I held the map up to show her. "Any recommendations on what to stay away from?"

Her forefinger came to rest on her lips and she tapped softly. "It's going to be easier to recommend places to go." She snatched the map from my hand without warning. She grabbed a pen from her purse and began circling and scratching off attractions. Under her breath she would say, "Not this place, but this one is all right. Can't forget this one. Definitely not."

When she was done, she returned the map to me. I was surprised to see so many attractions still on the list. "Thank you. I appreciate it. The...person that recommended I come here is a bit of a Wisconsin Dells fanatic."

She nodded. "Once you get away from the main strip, it's truly a beautiful place." When her phone chimed, she stared at the screen and sighed deeply. "I'm officially out of a job."

"They fired you through text? I've heard of getting let go through Zoom, but via text is cold. I'm so sorry, Alice."

"It's ok. I lasted longer than I thought I would. Luckily, I still live with my parents, so rent is reasonable," she murmured as she examined her shoes. "I hope you have a great rest of your vacation."

As she turned to go, I quickly asked, "Do you want to hang out with me? Show me the sights? I don't know anyone and you seem like you could use a distraction today, especially since I helped you lose your job."

Her face brightened. "It's not your fault. It is simply that you're the last customer I helped where I broke something. But I would love to hang out with you. Can I take a picture with you?"

With wide eyes, I shook my head.

"I wouldn't share it on social media. I don't have many friends on there anyways," Alice said and held up her phone in front of my face. Her account proved she had six mutuals. "Elaine and Marge are my mom and grandma. My grandma had social media before I did! The rest of them are my friends I've known for years."

"I appreciate that," I replied, "but we just met."

Alice blushed and then added softly, "Of course! I'm being so awkward. I'm sorry." She slipped her phone away and smiled at me. "Where do you want to go?"

Instantly, I liked Alice even more. Even if I hadn't been a psychic, I would have noticed her happy energy that exuded from her. Innocence and joy were hard to hide. "Where would you take someone who has never been here before?"

Her smile grew wide and she grabbed my arm. Alice zipped me around town and showed me the sights.

When both of our stomachs were growling at us, Alice recommended a small mac and cheese place because she had a buy-one-get-one-free coupon. "That's one of the perks of living here. There are always coupons," she said as she took a bite.

As we dug into our food, we chatted and I realized how easy it was to be around Alice. I didn't have many friends anymore. They had moved on to working the normal nine-to-five jobs, marriages, divorces, and children. I didn't even have a cat, and my job was far from normal.

Without warning, Alice had charged into my life and helped me when I was at a low point in my life. She didn't ask anything of me, outside of the photo, which I now felt guilty at denying her. Her phone had stayed tucked away in her purse all day, except when she answered a text message from her mother. I enjoyed being around her and didn't sense any maliciousness or ulterior motives. She was good for me.

Perhaps, I was good for her too. The moment she had taken me to experience the Dells, her anxiety seemed to drop dramatically. The care she took in choosing attractions impressed me. Our taste in activities appeared to be similar: candy shop, go-carting, and shopping.

"I appreciate you taking me around today. It was pleasant to get away from…my Dells-obsessed friend," I said.

"Of course! It was so much fun!" Alice replied, a huge smile spread across her face. "How long are you staying?"

With a sigh, I answered, "Probably another week."

"Well, if ever you want to hang out, I'm free. Every day. All day."

"Sounds like a plan," I replied.

"What's up with your friend? They didn't want to come out with you?" Alice asked as she grabbed her tray to take to the garbage. "Are they snobby about what they want to do?"

I followed her with my tray. "Bradley's not much of a people person. He's the type of person that likes the outdoors, but not the people that are around. He dragged me along on this trip, but for the first time since we got here, I'm having a lot of fun."

Alice faced me and lifted her eyebrows as she tilted her head to the side. She didn't say anything for a moment or two. "You sound irritated with him."

"Yeah. He's obnoxious," I replied quickly.

"Did you get in a fight?"

"Sort of," I answered hesitantly. I wasn't sure how much I wanted Alice to know about Bradley. Most people aren't comfortable around ghosts and get weirded out when I talk about them casually.

She pressed her finger to her lips and held it there for a

moment as if she had an internal debate. Finally, she asked. "Ok, hear me out. Is this Bradley a lover?"

"Ew. No," I said and could almost sense a dry heave coming on. "He's…we're…platonic. Buddies?"

"'Buddies,'" she asked while making air quotes with her fingers.

"He's barely a friend," I confessed.

"Then why are you on a trip with him?" she asked, confusion knitted in her eyebrows and forehead.

With a sigh, I said, "I've asked myself the same thing since the moment I met him." Then I shrugged and added, "He told me that I glimmer."

"Aww," she replied and then stopped abruptly. "That's an odd compliment."

"Well, he's kind of an odd guy."

Alice pursed her lips and shook her head. "You're leaving something out. Like some massive details about this guy. What is going on? I promise, I won't get weirded out. I have a friend who tells me all of her weird dating adventures. Makes me glad that I'm not on the apps," she rambled.

Inside, I was at war with myself. Alice had proven to be a caring and insightful person, but I had known her for less than twelve hours. Someone could pretend to be a lot of things for that amount of time. Hell, it took most relationships at least six months for their true selves to show to romantic partners.

But something deep in my gut had instantly bonded to this woman and the appeal of sharing a secret was too much to resist. There weren't many people I trusted with my secrets. No one knew about Bradley, not even my mother. It felt like it was burning a hole inside me and was desperate to get out.

"Let's get out of here," I told her. If I were to confess about the nature of how I acquired Bradley, I needed to be alone with her. We walked to a deserted side street and found a bench to sit on.

Alice studied me with her wide blue eyes but didn't say a word.

I sighed and opened my mouth to say something, but she interrupted me. "You don't *have* to tell me anything. It's not my business to know what's going on with Bradley, especially if it's causing this much internal struggle. If you ever want to tell me, I'm happy to listen. No judgement."

"Thank you," I replied. "So, to answer your question from earlier about what's going on with Bradley. He's a ghost I picked up and I'm not sure I like him. I probably don't."

Her hands came up to her mouth, and she asked with a muffled voice, "Where did you pick him up?"

"A rest stop." A number of emotions played across her face; confusion, bewilderment, surprise.

After a moment, she collected herself and stammered, "I…I didn't realize rest stops would be…haunted."

"In my experience, they're not usually. But Bradley is an anomaly." I filled her in on how I had acquired him and how he could travel with people.

She pursed her lips and asked slowly, "If you don't want him around, can't you send him to the light or something? Dispel him?"

I shook my head. "I've seriously considered it, but he's strongly against leaving this world. I may take off without him," I replied then sighed. "He died before he was ready and didn't get to do things he wanted to. I don't know much about him. He's closed off. Except he has a bucket list, and he won't share what else he has on it."

She dropped her hands and her lips made an 'O' shape. "Once he's completed it, is he going to leave this plane? Maybe you're the one who has to help him on his journey! There are tons of TV shows and movies about that happening."

"I hope not. Who knows how long his bucket list is. Or how expensive it will be. It's not like he'll be footing any of the cost for me to take him on these adventures," I said sharply.

"But can't you suggest that the studio do another show where they follow you around as you take him on these adventures?" she asked.

"I'm not sure the spotlight is for me," I replied softly.

"Really?" she asked, surprised. "I watched the first episode of your show a few times and it's wonderful. And in case you're wondering, I thought that way before I met you."

"Really?" Hope sprang in my chest. I had worked hard to get my show off the ground, and then my first run-in with bad publicity made me question everything. The moment I saw photos being taken of me at the beach, my entire outlook on the show had changed in an instant. I had forgotten that I had wanted the show in the first place.

"Really, really," she replied and her hand reached out to grasp mine. "You have an incredible gift. The way you manage people and spirits is impressive. I wouldn't be surprised if they sign you for another season."

I squeezed her hand. Did people come into our lives at the precise moment we needed them, like the old saying went? Or did I get a lucky break with Alice? It probably didn't matter which was true. "I won't pitch a new show right now. Not sure I want to hang out with Bradley indefinitely, much less for the length of a show. Hell, I can't even see him. Unless it's a half-hour special of me sending him off this rock."

Alice giggled. "Plus, how on earth would they pay him?"

I joined in her laughter and knew I had chosen wisely to share with her. It had been a long time since I felt a connection with another living person. "Thank you, Alice. You reminded me of why I went into this business."

As we got up from the bench, my phone chirped and saw a text message from my personal assistant, Laverna.

Laverna: Just checking in on you. Jack told me that you were off the grid.

Me: Yeah. Don't share my location with anyone.

Dots appeared on the screen to indicate she was replying, but a response didn't appear. When the dots disappeared without any message, I called her.

She didn't answer.

When her voicemail picked up, I said, "Laverna. I need you to tell me if you've told anyone where I'm at. Call me back."

I cursed at myself for not remembering to turn off my location on my phone. Immediately, I opened my phone settings to fix the problem. I turned off sharing my location. Earlier in the year, Laverna had asked me to share my location so she could find me whenever I needed her. Unfortunately, it appeared she had shared it with someone, especially if that someone was Jack or any of the tabloids.

Alice stood by my side, concern etched on her face, but she didn't pry. Then I realized she had heard everything and had deduced what was going on.

"Can I see your phone?" Alice asked.

"Why?"

"Just trust me, ok?" she answered with a sweet smile.

And I did. I handed her my phone, and she began tapping on the screen. The next moment, she handed my phone back and said, "I put my number in there for you. If you need me, you know how to get a hold of me. No pressure if you don't use it. But if there is ever a time I can help, I'll try my best."

My arms fell to my side, suddenly too heavy for me to hold up. The team that had been hired to make my life easier seemed to be doing everything in their power to ensure it was difficult. Then there was this woman who I had just met, and she was doing what she could to comfort me. It truly was the small things that mattered.

All I could muster to say was, "Thank you." But sometimes actions spoke louder than words. Quickly, I pulled her in under my arm and held up my phone. "Smile," I said. With a tap of my thumb, I took a photo with her. As soon as I took my arm off of her shoulders, I sent the photo to her without hesitation.

"See you later," I called to her as I walked back to my car. The sun had begun to dip toward the horizon, and it was time for me to go back to the motel for the night.

Five

Lost in the Fog

Someone whispered my name almost like a song. On the wind, the sound of an airy flute accompanied the voice. The door was open, and icy air spilled into the room. As I reached for the blanket, a wispy white hand grasped my wrist and tugged lightly.

I realized I was dreaming and smiled softly. There was nothing here that could harm me. Slowly, I got out of bed at the continued insistence of the hand. There was no body attached to it, but that didn't phase me. Weird things happen all the time in dreams.

Slowly, I let the hand guide me out of my room and into a cloud of dense fog. With the guilelessness of a child, I ambled into the night.

I had no sense of where I was being led or how far we had gone. On and on, the hand guided me. Anything nearby was hidden by the fog.

Slowly, the fog began to dissipate, and I began to see a road ahead of us.

The hand guided me down the deserted road as its grip tightened. Its pace increased with urgency.

The sky above me was clear. Millions of stars speckled the black sky. Goosebumps prickled on my arms as the chilly air grazed my skin.

My mind was blissfully empty. My constant internal chatter had been silenced.

When the hand's pressure and pace increased again, I struggled to keep up. My foot caught on a small rock and I tripped. Quickly, I recovered, but the hand yanked my wrist a second time. My feet struggled to stay underneath me. In an effort to get the hand to slow down, I pulled back against it. If they didn't slow down soon, I was going to fall.

I opened my mouth to tell them to slow down, but my words abandoned me. The only sound I could form was a croak that even I couldn't decipher what I had meant to say.

For what seemed like a mile, the hand led me ahead. I was disoriented and lost. It felt like I should know where I was, but couldn't find the location in my mind. Unease seeped into my mind, but I was helpless. The road seemed vaguely familiar, but the knowledge stayed hidden deep within my mind.

Without words, the message from the hand was clear. "Come. Come. We need you," rattled around in my head.

From out of the darkness, like a beacon, the white fence of the cemetery came into view. My heart slammed in my chest, and I finally knew where I was. My head shook back and forth as I shouted in my mind, "No!" But the hand only intensified its pressure on my wrist and pulled harder. An ache in my shoulder began to throb as it was tugged.

With a swift yank, I pulled my arm from the hand's grasp. For a second, I was free, but it found my wrist again. It's chilly grasp wrapped around my wrist and yanked me forward. When I stumbled again, I couldn't catch my balance.

Pain shot through my hands and knees as I hit the ground. Sharp rocks and gravel dug into my palms.

And the hand disappeared.

I blinked and realized I was awake, but I wasn't in my bed.

I wasn't in the motel.

I wasn't even inside.

The white fence of the cemetery was still ahead of me. The cool air blew over my skin and goose bumps traveled all over my body. Into the night, I whispered, "Bradley, if this is you, it's not funny." At least my voice was back.

No one responded.

As I got up, I tentatively touched the place on my wrist where the hand had grabbed me. The skin was icy, like the flesh of a corpse.

Inside the cemetery, small, white orbs of light flitted around the gravestones. The spirits within stayed back from the road and only peeked around the mausoleums, gravestones, and trees. On the breeze a dark sinister voice called my name. "Cassandra."

I took a step back and shouted, "I've seen enough horror movies and read enough faerie books to know not to enter an obvious trap. Especially when I'm brought here against my will."

The walk back to the motel took an unbearably long time. Rocks and dirt pricked my feet. My toes were painfully cold. My arms wrapped around me in a feeble attempt to warm my chilled skin. Over my shoulder, I yelled at the spirits, "Oh, and thanks for bringing me out here without shoes or a jacket. If I die of pneumonia, I'm blaming you!"

Finally, I reached my room and found the door had been left wide open. Despite my desire to slam the door behind me, it was late and I didn't want to wake anyone. Instead, I shut it gently but stomped my feet. Instantly, I knew that had been a bad choice. Pain shot through my feet. Between my painfully icy toes and the cuts that covered my feet from the gravel, I needed to be gentle.

In a whispered shout, I said, "Bradley, I swear to God, if you don't answer me right this second, I'm done with this road trip with you."

He grumbled before he replied, "Glad to see you, too."

"I need an explanation right this second. Either you influenced me in my sleep to go on a little midnight hike to that cemetery, or you saw me go and did nothing to stop it," I accused.

He sighed deeply and said, "I actually didn't do either of those things, thank you very much. I was on a walk. When I got back, you weren't here. How would I know if you meet a handsome fella…or lovely gal. My daughter always told me to be more open minded."

I stored away that he had a daughter. It would be something to ask him about another time.

My eyes rolled of their own volition. "But why weren't you here?"

"I figured you needed some space. Honestly, it seems creepy for me to sit watching you while you sleep. When you're heading to bed, I head out and do my sightseeing."

My anger at him began to dissolve. "I normally would appreciate that."

"Mind filling me in with what adventure you've been on tonight?" he asked softly.

Quickly, I ran through my dream and my journey up at the cemetery. "They want something, but they're going about it all wrong."

His deep sigh was followed by, "The spirits in the cemetery aren't welcoming. They don't seem to like me going into their space. It's not like I visited many cemeteries since I became a ghost, so I don't have anything to compare it to, but it's unsettling there. The spirits that belong there seem to barely tolerate the other spirits. Something guides me there, but as soon as I get closer the spirits tell me to leave. They warn me not to go inside, otherwise, I may never leave."

"That's odd. The whole place is odd. I'm not going in there," I said softly. "The thing is, I've never taken a spirit into a cemetery that wasn't residing there, so I'm not sure what they should act like. In my gut, I feel like they're acting wrong."

"I agree," he replied.

"You are an anomaly, Bradley. I'm surprised you were able to travel beyond the forest preserve you died at. In especially traumatic or unexpected deaths, they tend to stick to one place."

"It was like that at first, but as I said, I could move about with people that glimmered with light. In this place, I can move about relatively freely. I assume it's because..."

Quickly, I interrupted. "I radiate light. I do like to hear that."

He sighed again, "Yes. It's like you're a beacon and your ability lights the paths for me. I can go further than with anyone else I've ridden with before. Helps me get further away from you, which helps."

I began to wonder why Bradley was the first spirit to

tell me about the glimmer. I slowly realized the reason. Whenever a spirit approached me, it was for assistance, not for conversation. They used me as a way to resolve whatever problem still plagued them in the afterlife.

"Ha ha," but I didn't know if he was kidding. I felt like maybe he was. "You are the first spirit to tell me that I glimmer."

"Not surprising. The few spirits that I've met aren't the best conversationalists. 'Oh, boo-hoo, this,' and 'boo-hoo, that. They're so self-centered," Bradley replied.

I rolled my eyes and decided to not comment. Instead, I retreated into the bathroom and washed my hands and feet with a washcloth. Luckily, my cuts were minor and didn't need much attention.

Already, I knew that sleep would be evasive. The memory of being led by a hand sent a chill down my body, and all I wanted was to be under a blanket. I crawled back into bed and asked, "Bradley, would you stay with me tonight? Make sure I don't take off on another hike in the middle of the night? And please don't mess with the thermostat anymore. I'm still so cold."

He cleared his throat and replied, "Of course."

After flipping through a few channels on the TV, I settled on a rerun show I had watched a million times. The comforting sound of canned audience laughter and jokes I knew by heart calmed my nerves.

"You still there?" I asked softly.

"I'll be here all night," he replied softly.

Slowly, my eyes began to grow heavy and in moments I was asleep.

The morning sunlight peeked through the blackout curtains around the windows. With a quick stretch I called out to

Bradley, "You here?"

From next to me, he answered, "Been here all night. Nothing came in the past few hours."

"Thank you. I appreciate you keeping watch," I said softly.

He groaned softly and replied, "You're welcome. It wouldn't surprise me if they try another stunt on you sometime. They seem persistent. Since you're a psychic, can you use your sixth sense to understand the cemetery better?"

I nodded my head and closed my eyes. I reached with my mind's eye to the spirits within the cemetery. They pushed me away, even from this distance. When I opened my eyes again, I said, "The spirits don't want me there. They are too quiet. Perhaps, they've been silenced. I live across the street from a cemetery and they're the loudest group of…" I trailed off as an expletive was on my tongue. I got the sense that Bradley was about my dad's age. My dad would have chided me for what I had been tempted to say so I didn't push forward with Bradley.

"I know you weren't going to drop an F bomb, were you?" he scolded.

"Of course not," I said. After I sat up in bed, I added. "Last night you mentioned something about a daughter."

"You know, I'm not ready to talk about her," he replied.

"Can you give me something? Anything you'd like to share with me? I don't know you!" I said earnestly.

With a sigh, he answered, "I like to fish. Bass and trout fishing were my favorites. If you ever want to go to the store to pick out lures, I'm your guy."

For a moment, I waited for him to continue, but he remained silent. "Great. Anything more personal?"

"I suppose I could add that the best lure to catch trout are jigs. Can't go wrong with one of those," he announced proudly.

"I'll keep that in mind the next time I go bass fishing," I said flatly.

"Jigs are for trout. Not bass. Bass you need something else entirely. I prefer crankbaits for them," he replied.

I shook my head. "I guess I was hoping for something a bit more meaningful."

"You can't get much more personal or meaningful than when a man shares his preferences for lures. Just ask any fisherman," he said.

"Did you take your daughter fishing with you?" I asked, careful in my information gathering. .

"Nah. She didn't like the fish guts. We didn't have many shared hobbies. I wish she would have liked fishing. She was so chatty. Scared all the fish away. We never caught any fish when she was with me. Nothing like silence and the water," he answered wistfully.

I nodded. "It's tough when you have an expectation of how your day will go and someone interrupts those plans."

"Yep," he said softly.

After a moment of silence, I asked, "Do you have a favorite fishing spot?"

"Yep. Manistee River. Took my boat out as often as I could."

"That sounds nice. Did you ever take anyone with you fishing? Fishing buddy or anything?" I inquired.

"Nope. Didn't have fishing buddies," he sniffed. "Just me on my boat, Nimue, surrounded by nature That's when a man can really just think."

"The Lady of the Lake?" I asked. "You don't seem to be the Arthurian legend type."

"Nope, that would have been my daughter's idea. She chose

it from some book she was reading."

"She has good taste," I replied.

"I remember the day she named it. We were on the river and I caught a trout. She was only like five or something," he said with a tightness to his tone.

"Did you throw the fish back?" I asked softly.

"Of course not! It was an incredible trout. As soon as we were done, I rowed us back to shore and prepped it for lunch."

I shut my eyes as I imagined how his five-year-old daughter had reacted. "I'm assuming that is when her dislike of fish guts came in."

"Exactly! Maybe you're more talented of a psychic than you let on." He sounded astonished. "She refused to eat the fish. If I took her back to her mom hungry, I would never hear the end of it, so I had to grab her a cheeseburger from some fast-food joint."

With a shake of my head, I let the backhanded insult slide. He was sharing with me for the first time, and I didn't want to ruin the moment.

"After that, she would cry if I took her on the boat, so we had to sit on the shore. It wasn't fun after that, so I had to go by myself. I prefer being alone anyway," he replied gruffly. "Just me and the water."

"Have you always liked being alone?" I probed. Though he was sharing, it was like pulling each piece of information out inch by inch. I was working harder than he was and I wasn't even sure if he realized he was letting me in inch by inch.

"I'd say yeah," he answered simply and grew quiet.

We sat in silence. Regret poured out of him and filled up the room. He had finally shared some of his story with me. The weight of it fell hard onto me. My own regrets bubbled up inside of me and came to the surface. Where would my life have taken me if I had never met Zack? Would I have ever had the motivation to pursue a TV show?

As I was devoured by the what-ifs, my phone rang.

I groaned as I saw Jack's name pop up on my screen.

Thickly, Bradley asked, "Not someone you want to talk with?"

With a shake of my head, I held up the phone so he could see the caller ID. "The only person worse would be one of my ex-boyfriends."

With a groan, I answered. Jack didn't wait for me to speak before he jumped into talking at me. "Cassie, your show is a hit! You have to get back here. There's campaigning to do."

"Hello to you too, Jack," I said, my voice dripped in fake sweetness.

"Did you hear what I said? You need to get on these shows! I can probably arrange for a Wisconsin news station to interview you," he said quickly.

"Wisconsin? You know where I'm at," I said. My heart beat so hard that I could feel it.

"I do," Jack replied nonchalantly.

At that moment, I realized that while Laverna and I had a casual work friendship, money talked. Her loyalties didn't lie with me. Jack had hired her, which meant she would follow his directions. She had shared my location with him.

He continued, "There are things that are in your contract that you're obligated to do."

"I filmed the show. Even when we were negotiating, I told you I didn't want to do interviews," I reminded him.

"True, but no one would have agreed to that."

"What will happen when I don't do these interviews," I

snapped.

"I can't say for certain. I can talk about possibilities. You *could* lose your show for failing to follow through with your contract. There's always fines and fees you *could* incur. I know you're running to get away from people, but no matter where you are, people have cameras. Do you know how *easy* it is for someone to send a video to the tabloids? You're going to get recognized, with or without your location being shared," Jack said.

"I'm not doing them. You can't make me," I said.

"Don't make me do something you'll regret," he snapped.

Flames could have shot out my ears. It felt like everyone was using me. The spirits, the network, Jack, Laverna, and Bradley. They all had their uses for me, like I was a product. None of them recognized that I was just a woman who needed a break. It felt like I was carrying the weight of the world on my shoulders, and there was no one to offer me relief.

"Jack," I roared, but he interrupted me.

"Don't you dare entertain the fantasy that you could fire me without consequences," he snarled.

Would Jack send my location to the paparazzi? My palms began to sweat with fear that I would be photographed again.

When I was quiet, he shouted, "I expect you to be back here by the end of the week." Then he hung up.

Jack would share my location. It was only a matter of time.

Tears welled in my eyes and began to spill down my face. A tickling tingle traveled up and down my right arm and I knew Bradley was there.

We were silent and sat together for a long time.

When my tears had stopped, I wiped my cheeks dry. Bradley grumbled. "I believe it's time you stop running."

"What do you mean?" I asked with a sniff.

"You've done nothing but run since I met you. You're so scared of being recognized that you go out in a disguise. That man is holding all the cards right now. The worst part is that he knows it," Bradley replied.

Blubbering, I said, "Nothing has worked out the way I wanted it to. All I wanted was to get away for a bit."

Gently, he replied, "And I can see that you deserved that. I may have hindered your fun, but Jack would have found you wherever you went. If you had gone to some city, you wouldn't have anyone. At least here, you have support."

"What do you have in mind?" I asked.

"In my humble opinion, it is time you let the world know where you're at. Get onto your socials and get photographed having fun," he replied gently.

"Then he can't threaten that he's going to release my location. I'll have taken the power back," I replied with a nod.

"You'll control the narrative. If you can, get a group to hang out with you. Live people, not us dead folks. Unless you decide to do a ghost walk through the cemetery with a group. That would be on brand for you," he replied.

I grabbed my phone as I exclaimed, "I think I have the exact person to help with that."

Six

Annie & Molly

Thirty minutes after my text, Alice showed up at my motel door. She was wearing a pair of black distressed jeans with an oversized pink sweatshirt.

"Thanks for coming," I said as she came into my room.

"Of course!" Alice sat down in one of the two chairs near the table in the corner. She glanced around the room and asked, "How can I help?"

Without warning, Bradley piped in, "You should get a viewing party for your show set up at some local bar or restaurant."

Alice jumped up, her eyes scanning the room. "Who said that? Is that Bradley?"

I introduced them. "Alice, this is Bradley. Bradley, meet Alice."

Alice scanned around the room and hesitantly took a few steps toward the place she had heard his voice. Slowly, her hand reached out in front of her. "Can you see him?"

I shook my head. "No. Usually, new ghosts are invisible, even to psychics. He's coming up on his one-year death date."

Alice waved her hand in front of her, searching for him then she said, "Death date? Do you throw parties like you do for birthday's?" Suddenly, Alice yelped. "My hand turned cold and tingled!"

Bradley chuckled, and Alice jumped. "Watch where you're touching people, miss," he chuckled. "And no, I don't believe I require a death party. It was the worst day of my life. I don't need to be reminded of it annually."

"Sorry! That makes sense." Then with a shaky voice, Alice added, "It's…ni…nice to meet…you." She grabbed her phone out of her purse and snapped a photo where Bradley was standing. The shutter sounded and she quickly examined it. She sighed with disappointment and then shrugged. "Dang it! I thought that I'd be able to capture Bradley on camera."

"Can we get back to the problem at hand?" Bradley asked impatiently. "Cassie needs all the help she can get."

In a sarcastic tone, I replied, "Thanks, Bradley."

"Anytime. Now, Alice. I need you to help let the world know that Cassandra is here."

My heart jumped instantly at the thought of the ramifications. Even though I knew what needed to be done, it didn't stop my anxiety over what would be said about me. Or what other catastrophes would occur.

"Are you sure I'm the right person to help? Don't get me wrong, I'm happy to help any way I can, but I'm barely on social media. My grandma has a bigger presence than I do. I'm supremely unpopular," she said quickly. "I'm also confused by the change in plan, too. Yesterday, you didn't want to take a photo with me because you were afraid I would put it on social media. And now you want to let everyone know where you're at."

I nodded. "I know, but things have changed since then." I filled her in on the drama with Jack and updated her on the suggestions Bradley had made. Despite my fear, I smiled and asked, "How many friends can you get for a group hang?"

"If you think I can help you, I'll do my best." She reached into her pocket to pull her phone back out. Her fingers flew over the screen as she texted people. Almost immediately, her phone chirped with notifications.

"Great! My friends can make it! They're a lot of fun."

"What do you usually do for fun with them?" I asked.

Alice bit her lip before saying, "We play Dungeons and Dragons, mostly."

Before I could reply, Bradley said, "Dungeons and Dragons? Was that a part of the satanic panic in the '80's?"

"I think so," Alice said softly. "But it's not evil! It's just role playing. We each have a character that we play. Zander is our Dungeon Master and leads us through the adventures."

"So, you live in a fantasy world instead of living in reality?" Bradley asked with a sniff.

"Everyone needs a little escape from the real world," Alice replied.

"We're not…playing that today, are we?" I asked, stumbling over my words.

"No, of course not! We usually play in Zander's basement. That's not a great way to get you recognized. We're going to go out, have drinks, go do some of the attractions and give the impression that we're having a blast. However, I hope that we'll *actually* have fun instead of simply pretending," Alice said confidently. "Bradley, would you like to come with us?"

Bradley sniffed before he answered, "Absolutely not! There is no way in tarnation that I would be seen with a bunch of dullards running around pretending they're on an adventure."

"Woah there, Bradley," I replied. "You're whipping out the ol' tarnation. You're aging yourself there."

Alice smiled and added, "Plus, you're invisible. You wouldn't be seen with us."

With another sniff, Bradley replied, "Regardless, I have no interest in surrounding myself with more than one chatty person. My social battery is overfull from just Cassandra."

Alice and I looked at each other and shrugged. "Your loss," we said in unison. I grabbed my jacket, purse, and keys and we waved good-bye to Bradley. "*See* you later," we called over our shoulders.

A little while later, Alice and I arrived in the cute downtown square. Angel wings were painted on a wall nearby where people stood to get their photos taken. Sea glass standing art pieces were positioned throughout the area. Pergolas were sprinkled around. To me, pergolas were some of the most useless yard accessories. They didn't provide any shelter when it was hot or raining, but they were aesthetically pleasing.

Across the square, a gaggle of young adults walked with purpose toward Alice and me. Relief flowed through me, when I realized the group weren't in costumes and had followed Alice's instructions. Their outfits, however, stood out in a crowd

Alice jumped up and down when she saw them. Her hand flew like a bird into the air and flapped a wave to them.

Alice introduced the group to me. "Piper, Zander, Bear, and Hazel this is Cassandra Seer." Then in a whisper, she added,

"She's *the Emberford Psychic!*"

In unison, all of their eyes grew wide and their mouths dropped open. One of the girls asked excitedly, "We get to hang out with a celebrity?"

"Piper, be cool," Alice said as she flapped her hand at her. "We need your expertise especially. Cassandra's location needs to blow up."

Piper nodded in approval and her long, black box braids bobbed around her head. The tips of each braid were a rainbow of bright colors that matched her fitted rainbow dress. A bright rainbow heart made up the bodice. She could have stepped off the page of a magazine. Her deep brown skin was flawless. She had even created a dewy finish. I have never been able to accomplish that look. It didn't matter how many tutorials I watched, when I attempted, I always looked like I was sweating.

When the chatter had died down, Alice addressed the group for introductions. With one finger, she pointed to Piper, "This of course is Piper. Next we have Bear."

Bear nodded his head at me. His tan and defined muscles told me he spent time outside. Along with his dark red hair and beard trimmed neatly, he reminded me of a lumberjack. My heart fluttered as I wondered what exactly Bear did outside. Did he make wood chopping videos online for people to enjoy?

I would have expected him to wear a red buffalo plaid flannel top, but I sensed that would have been too traditional for him. Instead, he wore a long-sleeved shirt that had a cowl neck. The deep purple fabric wrapped around him tightly which allowed every muscle and curve to be enhanced. A silver buckle was placed near his right shoulder.

When Alice pointed at the other woman, she didn't wait for an introduction. "Hi! I'm Hazel. Huge fan!"

Hazel gave the impression that she should be frolicking through a field of wildflowers. The pastel pink dress with cream trim and lace she wore matched her pink buckled Mary Jane's. Her pale skin and wavy blonde hair shone in the sunlight. A cream lacy bow kept her hair from her face.

When Alice began to introduce the last member of the group, he interrupted her. "Alice, I can do my own introduction. I'm Zander," he said. His voice was rich and deep. My heart danced, and instantly I hoped that he was an audiobook narrator, especially if they were some exceptionally naughty books.

Zander wore a dark green hooded cloak, something like a hooded sweatshirt but with a cape sewn over it. His dark brown hair peeked out from under the hood. When the sun was freed from a cloud, its rays highlighted golden streaks in his hair that matched his skin. He was one of the most attractive men I had ever met.

It was not lost on me that I was significantly older than this group of people. They had to be in their early to mid-twenties. I was at least a decade older than them. I didn't want to be a cougar and decided to keep my thoughts on Zander and Bear's attractiveness to myself. They would be viewed only as younger brothers from that moment forward.

"It's nice to meet you all. I appreciate your help," I replied softly. "What are we doing first?"

Alice began to say something, but Zander interrupted her. "First, celebratory drinks so we can document your arrival at a local pub."

I turned to Alice and asked, "What was your idea?"

She blushed, but answered confidently, "I'm not sure alcohol is the best place to start. We don't need bad publicity for Cassandra. We need fun activities that would make great photos."

Under his breath, Zander added, "Alcohol is fun."

Alice lowered her chin and glared at him over her glasses. She chose not to reply to him directly and instead addressed the group, "How about we visit the deer?"

Hazel smiled and Piper nodded.

Bear's eyes never left Alice as he agreed, "That's a real winner of an idea." He shifted to stand closer to her. She blushed as she glanced at him with a tiny smile on her lips.

Zander sighed and said, "I'll drive since I've got the biggest vehicle. We can all ride together." He led us to his black Honda Odyssey minivan in a nearby parking lot. My face must have shown some confusion because he added, as he affectionately rubbed the hood of the van, "My mom knows how much room all of our extracurriculars take, so she got me this as a graduation present."

"That was a generous gift," I said. "Graduation from college?" I had done some mental math and thought that most of them were about the age to have earned degrees if they had gone.

Zander rolled his eyes and replied, "No. High school."

I nodded, knowing I had stuck my foot in my mouth. Impulsively, I asked, "What do you do outside of Dungeons and Dragons? Job? Influencer?"

"I wasn't put here to be a part of the rat race. What are we working for? Money? Status?" he answered fiercely. Then he unlocked the doors and got in.

Hazel tapped on my arm before I got in and whispered, "Zander's mom doesn't want him moving out and will do whatever he wants to keep him from leaving. She pays all his bills. I mean, if my mom did that for me, I'm not sure I would want to leave either.

Alice nodded and added, "His mom is really sweet, but spoils him. She doesn't want her only child leaving her as an empty nester. I think she's shy and doesn't have many friends."

***

When we were all seated and buckled, Zander drove us to our first destination. It was a deer park where we could feed a variety of animals.

Despite being situated next to a road, the rustic wooden fences and gates were a call back to the countryside. The grounds and land were tidy and well maintained. From the parking lot, we could already see some of the deer. Other patrons were already inside and many of them held out their hands to feed the animals.

Prior to that moment, I never had fervor about deer, outside of the fear of hitting one on the highway. The joy that bubbled up inside of me at the thought of getting to feed one made me feel like a child again. I eagerly paid my admission fee and led the group outside.

There were deer everywhere. Some enjoyed spots in the shade away from the noise and guests, while others positioned themselves near the feed machines.

A particularly large deer had found the perfect resting spot that was in the middle of one walkway. To avoid his wide antlers, guests had to walk around him.

Hazel was like a woodland fairy in her outfit. The surrounding deer completed the image. All she was missing was a pair of pink and white wings.

For a brief moment, I wished Bradley had joined me on this excursion, because I was sure the place would have made him nostalgic.

Bear handed me a feed cup, and I too, felt like I could have been an animal loving princess. Instantly, I forgot why I was there. I no longer cared how many people knew I was in the Dells. Being able to feed the deer and other animals became my utmost priority. And each animal deserved to be fed. It was now my mission.

They were calm, gentle, and obviously used to being handled by people. Their warm, wet tongues slurped up the feed from the palm of my hand. Quarter after quarter were pumped into the feed machines in an effort to ensure all of the deer were fed.

Piper and Bear took turns taking photos and videos, like they were my personal PR team. Then they would upload them to all their social media accounts. My phone began to chirp and chime with notifications as I was tagged in hundreds of photos. Quickly, I turned off the notifications so I wouldn't be bothered.

When a group of deer I had been feeding realized I was out of food, they moved onto another group nearby. I tossed the empty cup into a nearby garbage bin and wiped my hands on my pants. Around the property, I could hear birds and people calling to each other.

As I looked around me, someone at the back of the lawn attracted my attention. My group was scattered around feeding the deer and didn't notice me wandering away.

Against a fence, a pale woman leaned and watched guests visit the place. With a small smile, I nodded at her and walked toward her slowly. I joined the woman and leaned against the fence next to her. Her gaze didn't leave the guests, but she nodded to me. I followed her gaze, and saw what had her attention. A man in overalls was walking toward the main building.

"You have a wonderful place here," I said quietly.

In my peripheral vision, I saw her nod again. "Thank you. My children have meticulously taken care of our place here."

"It shows," I replied softly. "Is there anything I can do for you?"

She shook her head. "No. I'm not ready to go yet. I won't leave before my husband passes. I think I'm going to be here a while longer." Her pale arm lifted and she pointed to an older man who was refilling the crank feed machines. "I will stay here for him until it's his time to go. That way, we can go together into the great beyond, hand in hand."

"That makes sense. He's lucky to have you wait for him."

A ray of sun broke through the clouds and filtered through her. Light shone within her once solid form and gave her an ethereal glow.

"You are the first spirit here in the Dells that I've come across that has been willing to speak with me," I told her.

Her arms wrapped around herself and she shivered. "There's a chill in the air that wasn't there before. Something calls to me on the breeze, but I refuse to go. I won't go without John. Be careful. Whoever is doing the calling is only interested in mischief."

"I will keep it in mind," I said softly.

"Go back to your friends. They're going to get curious as to why you're talking to yourself."

With a smile and nod, I told her, "Have a great day, ma'am."

Alice had hidden behind a tree and stepped out as I walked back to the group. "You saw a ghost, didn't you?"

"Yes. I did."

A pair of deer walked up to us, but when we showed them our empty hands, they moved along to other visitors.

"Who was it? An owner? Was it someone's grandma who got run over by a deer?" she asked.

"Just a pleasant spirit that is watching over her family, animals, and grounds. I imagine she's one of the reasons this place is so serene."

Alice nodded and we walked back to the group. I wasn't ready yet to share the concerns the woman had shared. Maybe it was some strange anomaly that someone had brought with them on vacation and it would leave as quickly as they had arrived.

Seven

Heart & Souls

Hours later, Zander announced, "Alright. We've done all the things *you* wanted to do, but we need sustenance. Food and drink." Without waiting for a response or input from the group, he hit the gas and drove us off the beaten path to his favorite local dive.

The bar was dimly lit. Loud music played in the background. Zander walked to a table at the center of the room and sat down. It wasn't overly busy since it was a weekday. I guessed that the majority of patrons were locals.

He called to the bartender, "Eddy! We need a round of celebratory drinks! Whatever would be tasty!"

Soon, a waitress brought over a tray of shots and a handful of menus. "Here are some apple pie shots. Let me know if you need anything else." Each of us took a shot and drank them.

The alcohol didn't burn and did indeed taste like an apple pie.

"Anything else I can get you?" the waitress asked.

Zander, without opening his menu, answered for the group, "Yeah. We'll take two of the appetizer platters. And a round of New Glarus."

She quickly wrote down the orders and hurried away.

The friends chatted away while we waited for our food and drinks to be delivered to the table. Despite the fact that we had spent the entire day together, the group still had things to talk about. There was little I could contribute to the conversations around the table, especially with everyone having side conversations. Instead, I listened and observed them. As a person that witnessed people develop and maintain close friendships, but struggled to replicate them, I felt like an outsider.

My judgy inner voice answered, "They aren't your friends. After you leave this place you're never going to see or speak to them again. Besides, they're only using you because you're 'famous.'"

No matter how much I tried to talk back to the nasty comments I heard in my head, they persisted. My inner dialogue knew every weak point and struck with precision to cause the most pain and uncertainty.

When Alice said, "Hey!" she interrupted the barrage of insults my brain wanted to continue to sling at me. The chatter around the table stopped and everyone watched her. Her phone was in her hand, and a wide smile grew on her face. "Check your socials!"

In sync, we examined our phones and saw instantly what Alice was calling our attention to. While my phone had stopped notifying me hours before, my in app notifications were maxed out. Thousands of likes and follows met my eyes. Before the events of the day, I had around fifty thousand followers. Our activities had ballooned that number to over a hundred and fifty thousand.

The comments section was terrifying on a regular day, but there hadn't been a regular day for a while. With a deep breath, I took a peek at the comments. Instantly, I knew I shouldn't have ventured in. The first comment called me a charlatan.

I was about to turn off my phone again when Piper exclaimed, "Oh Cassandra, they love you!"

"I'm not sure which comments you found but the ones I saw were *not* of admiration," I replied.

"I ignore the negative and strictly focus on the positive. The negative will suck our energy like a vampire. And no one has time for that," Piper said as she held her phone out to show me her screen.

> *MamaDD44: Last year, I met Cassandra Seer (didn't know who she was at the time), but she told me that my mother was watching over my kids. She died when I was twenty and never met my kids. It's something I always wondered. She hugged me and I always remembered her. It was just a few weeks ago that I learned she was going to have her own reality show. Instant fan!*

After Piper took her phone back, I bravely glanced back onto my phone and searched for myself.

MamaDD44 had liked most of the photos I had been tagged in.

But for every MamaDD44 there were an equal number of people who were angry or disgusted by me or my ability. Unlike Piper, I could not simply skip past the negative comments.

It seemed those were the only ones I could find.

Giana3938: "Cassandra Seer is a fraud! She defiles God by claiming she can speak with the dead."

AnonymousUser93938262517: "I knew her in high school. Seems like that's where she peaked. She's very mid."

GaryWalterV: "Saw her today in the Dells. She didn't even talk to me, nor to the ghost of my mother that haunts me. Doubtful of her abilities."

TerryPollock: "She's gained weight."

Quickly, I turned off my phone. That had been a bad idea. My mother had always told me not to bother with the comment section online. That was where trolls waited to ambush you. Maybe my entire life was a bad idea. How could I believe that I would be able to handle internet hate when I struggled with hate from my town and community?

The group, however, seemed oblivious to the nasty comments.

"This one says they had never heard of you before they watched your show but loved it! They can't wait to see the next episode," Hazel exclaimed. Then her eyes grew wide. "Jamie Darling, long time crush of mine, sent me a friend request!"

Hoots and hollers erupted around the table.

Alice patted me on the shoulder when she saw my confusion. "It's no one you would know. Jamie is a bit...oblivious to Hazel's existence. Which, I'm not sure how anyone could be oblivious to her. She's simply fantastic."

I pointedly looked at Bear and Alice and wondered if anyone would say something about whatever was between those two. Alice seemed pretty oblivious to his attention. When no one bothered to point out the attraction between them, I shrugged.

Piper chimed in and added, "You've been in love with her for at least five years, right?

Hazel, instead of getting upset, smiled and said, "No. It's been 6 years, 3 months, and 8 days, exactly." Her tone turned dreamy as she continued, "When I saw her walk into our English class as a new student, she took my breath away. That was the only class we were in together and I was too scared to ask her out. I didn't know she would even remember who I was."

"She didn't know you when you were in school together," Zander mumbled, then took a deep gulp of beer.

Hazel's eyes grew large. "If she doesn't remember me from high school, why would she send me a friend request?"

Piper shrugged. "From where I'm sitting, I don't see that it matters so much. Just ask her out now. You've waited long enough."

Hazel took a drink from her beer and sent a message to Jamie. Almost instantly, Hazel jumped out of her seat. "She said yes to a hang out!"

Zander gave her a high-five and congratulated her.

"Hey Alice? What about you? Do you have anyone you're interested in?" I asked. As soon as the words left my mouth, I wished I could take them back. Why was I trying to stir up possible drama? Maybe it was the beer that influenced me to throw out a question like that in front of the whole group. A small timid voice inside my head thought, *'Or you've found people that make you comfortable.'*

Bear took a deep drink from his bottled beer, but his eyes didn't leave Alice. She shrugged, oblivious to Bear's observations.

"Not at the moment. Why? Have you heard of someone who likes me?" she asked. "I could like them!"

Piper rolled her eyes. "Alice, you do *not* have to fall for someone simply because they say they like you." She scrutinized Bear and tilted her head toward Alice, but he dropped his head and suddenly found his beer intriguing.

Piper shrugged and grabbed another mozzarella stick.

Zander's eyes were glued to one of the large TVs that were arranged around the room, where most of them showed the same game. "Hey, Cassie?" he asked.

"I'd prefer to be called Cassandra."

"*Cassandra*. When's the next episode of your show airing?" He asked.

Before I could answer, Hazel interrupted. "Next Wednesday. Nine, Eight Central."

Zander ran a hand through his hair and twisted a lock. He was quiet for a few moments before he announced, "You should do a viewing party of your show."

Alice perked up and replied, "You know, Cassandra's friend mentioned the same thing!" I pleaded with my eyes that she would not mention that the friend was in reality a ghost.

Hazel added, excitedly, "If there is a lot of interest, we could do a pub crawl to some of the bars that would be willing to show it and Cassandra can stop by each one to make an appearance."

Hazel was on her phone again. "Eddie's Bar is on board."

My heart began to pound in my chest, and my palms began to sweat. "I…I…don't know if we need to do all that. This is enough here."

Hazel shrugged. "Too late. Molly's and The Moose have agreed to be on the bar crawl."

"How many bars are in this place?" I asked, my voice raising a few octaves.

"A lot. My dad works at city hall, so he knows all the business owners. I go along with him to build community relationships with them bi-weekly," Hazel said.

Alice wrapped an arm around me and squeezed me. "We'll be with you every step of the way. You're not going to do this alone."

Simultaneously, all of our phones made noises. The screen on my phone lit up with notifications from events Piper had tagged me in on all of her social media pages. While we had all been talking, she had quietly and quickly made an event, created a flyer, and invited a hundred people to it. Already, there were ten people that had RSVP'd yes to the event.

Piper waved her hand as if she was brushing away something in the air when she saw the awe on my face. "I'm a social media content creator for my job. In college, I studied marketing."

"No offense, but you stay here?" I asked. "Wouldn't it be better somewhere like a city or something?"

Piper shook her head slowly, as if she were about to educate a grandmother who had said something incredibly old-fashioned. "I work for major corporations remotely. I can live where I want, and this is where I want to live."

My head dropped in embarrassment. I always forgot about remote jobs, probably because I didn't have any skills that would be useful online. "Sorry about that."

"Don't worry about it. I have to remind my mom all the time when she brings up my career," Piper said.

While I wasn't old enough to be her mom, unless I had been a young teen mom, her comment gave the impression that I should have a candy bowl somewhere at home filled with some of those strawberry candies. Maybe a pack of wet wipes as well.

The night was getting late, my social battery was full, and I wasn't sure how much more embarrassment I could take that night.

"Thank you everyone for your help today. I had a lot of fun," I said as I rose from my chair.

The rest of the table got up in agreement, and we left the bar.

Outside, it was dark and chilly. I shivered as we began to walk to the parking lot. The group chatted behind me about how cold it had turned since we had entered the bar.

Then a cry rang out. Across the street, there was a densely wooded lot where a river ran nearby. Instantly, my ears pricked, and I stopped in my tracks. With closed eyes, I listened for the sound again.

"Did you hear that?" I hissed.

Zander shook his head and continued to chat with the others. Their noise obscured any sounds. "Shh!" I hissed.

The group hadn't heard me, and they continued to chatter and laugh. Quickly, I walked across the street and stopped at the edge of the woods and listened again for the cry. If I could hear it again, maybe I could tell if it was a human or animal. But the woods were quiet.

"What's up, Cassandra?" Alice yelled as she ran to catch up to me.

"I heard something out there. Like a cry," I said, pointing to the woods.

"It's not safe to go in there, especially at night," she replied.

The rest of the group caught up to us. Zander leaned onto Piper's shoulders and said, "I wouldn't recommend going into the woods, especially when you're not familiar with the area. You know, Bigfoot is in there, right? I should know. I am the president of our local Bigfoot spotting group."

The cry came again and everyone fell silent as they listened.

Without a second thought or warning to the others, I ran into the woods. I knew with certainty it wasn't an animal. "Call again! I'm coming," I yelled to whoever was in there.

Behind me, I could hear the group call after me. "Cassandra! Where are you going?"

I didn't have time to respond as I disappeared into the night. Almost immediately, I had to jump over a large fallen log and dodge a pile of cut wood.

There was no thought in my head except, "Go! Now! Hurry!" I raced further into the woods and ignored the group behind me. My speed increased with each step. I had never felt more confident in my agility before.

To my right a child's voice cried, "Help! I'm over here!"

Behind me, the others had heard the child. Hazel yelled out, "Spirits that sound like children could be demons!"

I veered toward where I had heard the child's voice and dodged a few trees in the nick of time. Running through the woods at night wasn't the safest activity. Even the bright moon was obscured by the canopy above. Where the light broke through, it allowed me to see some of the objects nearby. My reflexes were on point, and I jumped over a hole at the last minute.

Something told me that even if I had been running in full darkness, I would have been compelled to take the same path.

At a break in the canopy, a ray of moonlight fell upon the ground and highlighted a child. Huddled near a tree was the small form of a little girl. She was curled on the ground with clothing covered in mud. Violently, she shivered. I was surprised she had been able to call out.

"I'm Cassandra," I said as I slipped off my sweatshirt and wrapped it around her body. Quickly, I got on the ground and pulled the girl into my lap and rubbed my hands up and down her arms, my feeble attempt to try to warm her. She needed to get out of the cold now. Her lips were tinged blue. Her icy fingers touched my face for a moment, and I could see they too were beginning to turn blue.

With teeth chattering, the girl replied, "I…I'm…Vi…Violet." She leaned into me as she vibrated with shivers.

To the group somewhere still lost in the woods, I yelled, "Call 911!"

Eight

Here Before

By the time I fell into bed exhausted, it was 3 a.m. My impromptu excursion in the woods now made my entire body feel weak and shaky. I had never been a runner, even when I was younger.

The police had arrived first, quickly followed by an ambulance. We could see their flashlights as they approached. Bear had tried to take Violet from me, but I refused. Something told me I had to keep her in my arms until she could get into the ambulance.

As soon as the EMT's found us, they ripped Violet from my arms and took her into the warmth of the vehicle. At some point, a thermal blanket was wrapped around my shoulders and an EMT guided me to another ambulance to get checked out. Luckily, it only took them a few moments to realize that I was not suffering from any ill effects from the elements.

As I was released from their care, local news stations showed up, their cameras took in all the activity, with me in the center. I overheard one reporter say, "We are getting confirmation that the woman that assisted in the rescue of the missing child, Violet Chandler, is TV Psychic, Cassandra Seer. It is still uncertain if her abilities were used in locating the girl. According to her recent social media posts, she's been vacationing here in Wisconsin Dells."

In a blur, I found myself with the police.

A female police officer asked, "How did you find the girl?"

"I'm not...," I said, but then stopped mid-sentence so I could watch the ambulance that carried Violet drive away. She would get medical attention and be reunited with her family at the hospital.

The officer asked me questions and I answered them, but fatigue was in control, and as soon as I answered a question, I forgot what they had asked. When they were satisfied with my account, they released me, and I was free to go. My friends huddled near the news cameras.

One reporter called out to Alice, "Miss! Can you tell us what happened?"

Wide-eyed and fingers playing with her painted nails, Alice slowly walked up to the group of reporters. She nodded.

Microphones with the numbers of several local news stations were placed in her face. In the sea of reporters, someone asked, "What's your name?"

"I'm Alice Triggs. My brave friend, Cassandra Seer is a hero. She ran into the woods, without knowing the land or who was crying out. She risked her safety without fearing consequences for herself. We were leaving Frank's bar and were walking back to our car when she heard the little girl. We," she rambled and waved her hand at the group, "all live here, and she raced ahead of us. She doesn't even live here! Or know these woods. She ran in without concern. Within a few moments, we lost her. It wasn't until she yelled for us to call 911 did we finally find her."

A balding man who was holding a Channel 29 microphone asked, "How did she find her?"

"How doesn't seem like the principle concern right now. What does seem crucial is that Violet is alive. I witnessed Cassandra's incredible navigation in a dark wooded area. She rushed in and somehow missed all the trees, fallen branches and any holes. She found the exact spot that Violet was. I know that little girls' parents are able to hug their daughter tonight thanks to the *Emberford Psychic*," she said.

A barrage of other questions rang out, but Bear shook his head and pulled Alice away from the reporters. As soon as she was within reach of the group, they pulled her into their ranks, and they left the reporters behind. When they got close to me, I felt their arms wrap around me and pull me into a group hug.

"I'm tired. Will you take me to my motel?" I asked the group.

Collectively, they all exclaimed, "Yes!"

We were silent as Zander drove us. I believe they could all sense the exhaustion pouring out of me. It had been a full day and even more eventful night. As soon as Zander parked his van outside my motel room door, Bear jumped out and ran around to open the van door for me. His warm hand reached out for mine and he helped me down. Gently, he took the key from my hand and opened my room for me.

With an exaggerated bow, he held his hands out as if to show me the way to my room. "Thank you, kind sir," I whispered and took the key from the lock. Slowly, I waved to the group and shut the door behind me.

"Bradley, if you're here, please avert your eyes," I instructed as I stripped off my clothing. If I hadn't been covered in dirt, pine needles, and mud I would have preferred to have collapsed in bed.

Instead, I quickly threw on a pair of pajamas and promptly fell face first into bed. A shower would have warmed me, but the threat of falling asleep while under the water was a real worry. I didn't have a desire to drown in the bathtub. Who knew how many boob photos would be released then?

A moan released as my body melded into the soft mattress beneath me.

"All clear?" Bradley asked.

"Yes," I answered.

"If I'm not mistaken, you've had an exciting night, young lady," Bradley said.

Without lifting my head, I waved him away. "Not now. Soo tired. Sleep, sleep time."

"You've been drinking," he declared close to my face.

"Yup. Sleep, sleep, Bradley. No more talkie for me," I replied in a babyish voice.

Bradley grumbled from across the room. "Well, get some sleep then. Tell me all about it in the morning."

***

I closed my eyes for a second, and when I opened them, it was morning. The clock on the bedside table read that it was 11 am. With a yawn, I stretched my arms and legs out as far as they would go. When I pointed my toes, a sharp pain shot through both of my feet.

After I sat up, I pulled my feet closer to me so I could inspect them. Across the bottoms, cuts, slivers, and gravel bits were embedded into them. "But I wore shoes when I found Violet,"

I said out loud. "Bradley! Did I go walking last night?"

There was no answer.

"Bradley?" I called again as I plucked the rocks from my feet. When I was sure there was nothing else I could pick out, I carefully got up and hobbled to the bathroom to clean the wounds. Without bandages or gauze, I used tissues to press onto the few spots that were bleeding.

"Bradley?" I called again. He didn't reply.

Quickly, I put socks on my feet to hold the tissues in place. I didn't even have tape to keep the makeshift gauze attached to my feet. As soon as I had new clothes on, I felt the urge to venture outside. Gingerly, I walked down the driveway toward the road.

Without thought, I headed to the cemetery again. My feet were in charge and quickly took me where they wanted to go, despite the ache radiating from my legs. "Why do the spirits in the cemetery keep trying to get me to go to them?" I said out loud to myself. "I bet they won't talk to me again, even once I'm there."

The moment I crossed the street to stand in front of the entrance, a shiver ran up my spine. The number of spirits inside the cemetery was overpowering. Spirits hovered throughout the cemetery and peeked out from behind trees, gravestones, and the mausoleum.

Between now and the last time I had stood outside of the fence, the number of spirits had at least tripled. There were far too many within the space. It felt unlikely that the underworld would have maximums on the number of spirits that could occupy the same space, but it couldn't be comfortable for them. I had never asked, so I couldn't be sure.

For myself, I knew that having that close proximity to the

high number of spirits in the cemetery would overwhelm me, even if I was a spirit. It's supposed to be a time of peace and rest for the soul. The cemetery felt anything but that.

A healthy cemetery would always have spirits around. It should have the newly passed and older spirits, who I viewed as guardians of the land and welcomers to the newly departed. Of course, the personalities of the spirits would differ widely, and there was always at least one cranky ghost. I knew when my grumpy neighbor, Mrs. Koch, died, she would be the cemetery curmudgeon.

So, unless the Dells and surrounding areas had experienced a massive event that killed a ton of people, I doubted that all the spirits belonged there. It truly felt like it was bursting with spirits.

"Bradley!" I called out.

A whisper like music on the breeze brought a smile to my lips. I took a step forward. It wasn't Bradley, but someone was beckoning me to visit.

Slowly, I took a few more steps until I was inside the property line. Trees stood in small groups around the lot, giving ample shade throughout on sunny days. Today was overcast with the sun hidden behind thick, gray clouds. Tendrils of fog crept along the ground, parting for the stones.

With each step I took, the spirits inside retreated further back from me.

This wasn't normal. Most of the time spirits and ghosts were drawn to me.

"Why do you keep bringing me here and then refuse to talk to me?" I shouted.

No one answered.

Behind headstones and mausoleums, spirits peeked but

never approached. Their silence was deafening.

What had happened to them? Outside of knowing there were so many spirits in one space, there wasn't a sense of anything inherently evil or malicious.

When in the presence of spirits, it was common to experience sadness, from them and within myself. But here? It was missing. The place was devoid of all emotions.

The only word I could grasp from them was hide.

"Cassandra!" someone called behind me.

As I turned to see who had yelled my name, the spirits retreated further until I couldn't sense them anymore.

Alice hung out of the window in a rusted brown car. She waved frantically. "What are you doing?" she called.

Slowly, I walked away from the headstones and approached Alice.

Once I was closer to her I answered, "Hey. I took a morning walk. Why are you hanging out of the window? Last time I checked, cars have doors."

She blushed and scratched her forehead. With a nervous giggle, she said, "Yeah, but this hunk o' junk doesn't open on this side. I have to climb over the passenger seat to go through a door. One time my uncle, Wayne, had to jimmy the door open and it hasn't been the same since."

"So, what's up?" I asked.

"You didn't answer your phone. Social media is blowing up, so I decided to take a drive over to see you. When I got to your room I found that the door wasn't shut all the way. After I peeked my head in and saw your keys, phone, and purse were all still there, I panicked. I drove around the parking lot to see if you'd gone for ice or something, but you weren't there. So, I decided to drive around to see if I could find you. That's when

I saw you walking around the cemetery," she said, her words quickly tumbled out of her mouth.

Whatever had held my attention and thoughts before snapped off and I realized I was shivering. When I had left, I hadn't grabbed a sweatshirt and only had my pajamas on. There hadn't been a moment of consideration to grab anything, much less change into warmer clothing, before I had left the motel.

Alice slipped into her car, reached across the passenger seat and opened up the side door. "Get in!"

I ran around the car and hopped inside. She cranked the window shut and blasted the heat. "Almost nothing extra works in this car, except the heat," she said, warming her hands by the vent.

As we drove back to the motel, a constant buzzing and chirping came from the back seat. Alice reached behind her and pulled out my purse. "Hope you don't mind, but I put your keys and phone in there. I didn't want anyone getting into your room and taking anything."

"Thank you," I replied and rifled through my purse until I found my phone. Notifications had been silenced overnight, but now at nearly noon, the quiet hours on my phone were null and void. Thousands of alerts from emails, texts, and social media demanded my attention. Of course, my family had seen the news.

Dad: I thought you were supposed to be on vacation. Just like your old man - when you're called to duty, you answer. Get some rest today.

Mom: I'm not calling you because you need to be resting.

Your gifts brought you to that little girl. I'm proud of you. I just wish you were getting some R&R, like you need. Please call me after you've had some sleep to let me know what happened.

Mom: I love you.

Ilona: Of course you make the news. At least you didn't die in the woods. If you did, we'd set you up as our basement ghost.

Diana: Mom was ready to head up there last night. I reminded her that she has two other daughters that don't keep her awake at night. Prematurely aging her. She got a new wrinkle yesterday. I watched it form. That's all on you. Love ya!

I rolled my eyes at my sister's texts. They poked fun at me all the time. That's what older sisters did, right?

In the family chat, I answered them.

Hey Dad! I am having a wonderful time, outside of last night. There wasn't a lot of thought, obviously, when I ran into the woods. Lucky for me, I found her relatively quickly. Only rest and fun for me today. Cross my heart.

Hey Mom! I'm sorry to make you worry. I'll try not to do that again...this trip. I'll send pictures to show proof of life.

Diana & Ilona, as always, your care and concern is

overwhelming. If I concentrate extremely hard, I can tell you love me.

With a sigh, I turned to social media. Despite my best effort to not care about what others thought of me, I did care. I wanted to be liked. Plus, the more people who liked me, then maybe my show would get renewed. With a few days between the seagull/bikini top incident and now, I realized that it was paramount to me.

The response from the world was overwhelming. While it had been a happy accident that I had found Violet, that act had helped people form an image of me. Overnight, I had acquired another fifty thousand followers.

With apprehension, I peeked at the comments left on my feed and posts. Almost instantly, the anxiety waned. A majority were positive. When I came across a negative comment, I scrolled on and searched for a more affirming one.

Luckily, the responsibility of responding and managing the comment section did not fall onto me. Laverna had written clever responses to posts I had been tagged in. Her most essential task was to block and delete truly horrific responses and comments.

Email notifications let me know that I had almost a thousand unread. I shook my head and thought, *"Who even likes emails? They are soul crushing."* Our ride was short. As we parked, I happily ignored the emails. They would be next week's Cassandra problems.

When we were back in my room, I grabbed my sweatshirt and pulled it over my head. Alice shut the door behind us and planted herself in front of me.

"What exactly is going on?" she asked.

I shrugged. "Nothing. Can't someone go for a walk whenever they want without being interrogated?" I replied unconvincingly.

"Without shoes? There's blood mixing in with the dirt on your socks," Alice said. She shook her head and added, "It's a good thing for you that I have a first aid kit with me." Without another word, she turned and went to her car. In moments, she was back and instructed me to sit down on the chair. As I peeled my socks off my feet, she said skeptically, "So you were taking a walk?"

I shook my head and knew I had been caught in my lie. If I had attempted to lie to my sisters about what was going on they would have called me on my bullshit. "So, here's the thing. I wasn't out for an *intentional* walk, meaning I had no conscious choice in going for a walk. There's something in the cemetery that, for a lack of a better word, keeps manipulating me to go there."

She gasped as she handed me a washcloth to wipe my feet. "How many times has this happened?" Her voice told me that she knew I wasn't a fraud.

As I cleaned and tended to my feet, I replied, "Three. The first time, it influenced me to walk there shortly after I got here. When I realized what was happening, I yelled that I wasn't going in there. Since then, they come to me when I'm sleeping. After I got back last night, they compelled me without my knowledge. And now that I'm reflecting on it, I believe they influenced me again to go this morning. So, four. Also, Bradley is gone."

She looked around as if she would be able to tell if he was missing and asked, "How long has he been gone?"

"It's hard to tell with him being invisible and a sulky, grouchy, old man," I answered. "He was here last night, and this morning he was gone and my feet had cuts on them."

"Well, that settles it. It's not safe here. You're going to come stay at my house," she said without hesitation.

Shaking my head, I replied, "No. The smart thing to do *would* be to get out of here and go back home. But that would be another thing taken out of my control. Sure, this isn't the vacation that I had envisioned. Bradley fundamentally hijacked me, but it's turned into something more incredible than I could've imagined. Getting to meet you and your friends has been a highlight. Besides, I've paid the money to stay here and I'm not going to give up anything else on this trip. My mother didn't raise a quitter."

Alice nodded her head and said, "I wish you would reconsider. The invite is always open. Is there anything we can do to keep you safe?"

"We need a rock shop," I replied.

She pointed to the door, "There's a place we can mine our own rocks, if that's what you're talking about."

"No. I need one of the shops I saw my first day here," I insisted.

Alice nodded. "Yeah, we can hit those places up. I'm sure they have what you need."

"Do you know anywhere we could snag some holy water?" I asked.

"There's a Catholic Church like four minutes from here," she replied.

"Are they open?" I asked.

"Do churches close? Do they even sell holy water?" she asked.

I shrugged. "I wasn't planning on buying."

Nine

Kodo & Podo

"Do we honestly want to do this?" Alice asked as she walked slowly behind me. Under her breath, she mumbled, "Why did I tell you about the church *my* family attends?"

"You told me because you're familiar with the layout. We'll be in and out in moments. I'm sure no one will even notice we're there," I called behind me.

After we parked in a nearby parking lot, the spire of the church peeked out from the trees and buildings. I quickened my pace. The sooner we could get this done, the better. A few minutes later we stood outside the church's pair of red doors. From the building, we could hear parishioners' voices in song. Alice's eyes were wide as she shook her head. "No. We're not doing this." Her arms crossed over her chest in protest.

I nodded and pulled open the door by the gold handle. "Yes we are," I whispered.

A mass service was underway, and the congregation filled the pews. Many of their heads were bowed in prayer. At the altar, a group stood around a marble pedestal that I assumed held holy water. A woman held a baby who wore a pristine white gown.

As quietly as we could, we snuck inside and tried to blend into the background.

Pointedly, Alice held my gaze and whispered, "We're not going to go up there and take it right? There's a baptism happening."

I shook my head, turned my back to the congregation, and pointed at the marble wells on either side of the entrance. Quietly, I replied, "There's holy water right there. We'll simply syphon it off here. Easy Peasy."

She moved to one while I approached the other. Slowly, we filled up the vials while the priest led the congregation.

My second vial was almost full when I heard a clang! The sound echoed throughout the vaulted ceilings and interrupted the song the congregation had begun to sing only a moment before.

Startled, I jumped and searched for the source of the sound. Alice, red cheeked, bent over to retrieve a metal water bottle that had escaped her bag and clattered to the marble floor.

Every single eye in the place turned around to see our fingers in the holy water and vials in our hands. The priest held a hand up to us and beckoned us forward.

Loudly, he called to us, "Good afternoon! Please join us."

Alice's hands shook as she stoppered her vial. She slipped both the vial and the water bottle into her bag.

Then we bolted and threw open the double doors.

With a vial full of holy water clenched in my fist, we raced down the cement stairs. Our faces were flushed with more than exertion. The embarrassment of what had happened would never leave me. I could only imagine how bad it would be for Alice. At least her mom wasn't there to witness the event.

By the time we hit the bottom step, someone ran out behind us. We slowed down enough to hear a man yell, "Alice Triggs! You could've just asked Father Michael for some holy water. He has a ton in the back!"

Alice waved a hand behind her and he added, "Does your mother know that you're *stealing* from the church? Wait until she hears about this!"

Quickly, I shoved the vial in my hand into my purse and grabbed her arm to stop her from responding to the man. We ran away and didn't stop until we got back to my car. I zipped out of the parking spot and drove straight to my motel room. Only when we were inside, the door shut and locked behind us, did we begin to catch our breaths. Together, we collapsed on the bed.

"I can't believe," I said, "you dropped your water bottle. Why did you bring it?"

Alice winced and replied, "I always have a water bottle with me. Doesn't everyone?"

"Maybe keep it inside the bag and not in one the shallow pockets on the outside," I said.

At least I never had to step foot into that church again, but poor Alice lived here and they knew who she was. And they knew her mother.

After fifteen minutes of rest, we finally caught our breath.

Alice said, "I can't believe we stole holy water."

"Girls are gonna be girls," I replied. "Now, we need to go get some rocks, crystals, and salt."

Alice smiled and asked, "Like iodized salt?"

"That would work in a pinch, but I'd prefer Himalayan salt."

She rolled off the bed and grabbed me by the arm. With more strength than I would have guessed she had, she pulled me up out of the bed and out to my car.

As we waited to pull onto the street from the parking lot, I felt the urge to turn left toward the cemetery. With every fiber of my being, I resisted but struggled to turn to the right. My arms refused to obey.

With deep breaths, I tried to slow my panicked breathing, but neither the breath nor my arms obeyed.

"The road is clear," Alice said. "Did you forget something?"

I shook my head, then I gasped.

On the road, twenty or thirty spirits appeared. They bobbed up and down as they slowly floated toward the cemetery. Sunlight cut through their transparent bodies.

Alice examined the road ahead of us and asked, "What is it? Do you see something?"

Of course, Alice couldn't see the spirits. "I know where Bradley has gone," I replied. "There's something in that cemetery that's collecting spirits. There's a group of them right in front of my car. I'm waiting for them to pass by. It would feel…disrespectful to drive through them."

Alice picked up her phone and tried to take some photos, but when she sighed in disappointment, I assumed she didn't capture anything.

"It would be difficult to get a photo when it's so light outside," I reminded her.

"True," she said sadly. "Do you need me to drive? That cemetery is bad news, and you don't need to go there."

I attempted to turn right again with the steering wheel, but my hands refused to move. They desperately wanted to turn left though. With a nod, I replied, "Please drive. I don't want to go there either."

As soon as I got out of the car, my feet began to take steps toward the road. Alice raced to me and said, "Nope. You're not going there today."

With her hands pressed down hard on my shoulders, she guided me to the passenger side of the car. She didn't move until I had buckled my seatbelt. Quickly, she ran to the driver side and locked the doors once she was in the seat. There was a draw to open the door and jump out. "We need to get out of here, now!" I said quickly.

Alice didn't seem to be affected by whatever was in the cemetery and pressed down on the gas. She turned right and sped down the road, away from the cemetery and toward the downtown area.

After shopping at a few stores, I was able to purchase black tourmaline, obsidian, and an amethyst. The Himalayan salt was a bust.

"I guess we need some iodized salt," Alice stated with defeat.

"Are you ok if we go back to the grocery store?" I asked hesitantly.

Her strained smile told me she wasn't.

"I've got an idea. How much salt do we need?" she asked brightly as she led me back to my car. When I approached the driver's side, she shook her head and pointed to the passenger side. "You're the passenger princess today!"

Over the next hour, she drove me to as many fast-food restaurants as we could find. At each stop, we rushed in and raided their condiments area to search for salt packets. We grabbed as many as we could without depleting any single establishment and spread the salt nabbing throughout the Dells. After each stop, we stashed the packets into an empty paper lunch bag I found in the back seat.

When the bag was about half full, I wasn't convinced we had enough yet. Estimation wasn't a strong skill of mine and I never guessed correctly when there were contests to write down how many gumballs were in a jar. Tiny salt packets in a paper bag were no easier. "How much salt is in each of those?" I asked Alice.

She reached into the bag and pulled out a packet to examine it closer. She shrugged. "It doesn't say. Let me check online." She opened her phone and then announced. "There are about .5 grams in each and there are 737 grams in a full container of salt."

"That's going to mean an awful lot of packets," I whined.

She thought for a moment and then excitedly announced, "We only need 1,474 packets!"

I shook my head. "We don't have that, do we?"

"Nope, but that's ok! We'll need to step up our game. Let's go find some more places," Alice said cheerfully. "This is the most fun I've had in a while."

"Petty theft will do that to you," I replied.

Her light laughter and smile came before she answered. "Could be the running that is raising my heart rate and bonding me to you."

I nodded. "Could be. But whatever the reason, we're not done today." "Let's hit the road!," Alice cried.

She drove me to a local restaurant and sat in a booth. We looked around and spotted full saltshakers on either side of us. Alice smiled and reached into her purse to pull out the paper bag. She set it on the seat next to her.

Then we browsed the menu.

When the waitress had taken our order, we waited until our food was placed in front of us before we started pilfering. Alice grabbed one from a neighboring table while I did the same. Then we emptied the saltshaker into the paper bag.

We ate a bit and added more salt into the bag, alternating between eating and stealing. Only when the contents of three saltshakers had been added into the bag did we finish eating. I left the tip for the waitress, but Alice added a few extra dollars. "I'm repenting for taking their salt," she announced.

Back at my motel room, we sat at the small table and chairs and began opening the salt packets into the lunch bag. When they were all opened, Alice counted the packages. The bag of salt sat nearby.

Alice whispered, "We opened 974 packets of salt. It's fortunate that we got the salt from the restaurant. Now what are we going to do with this? Warding spell? Call on guardian angels? Raise our own sexy vampire to take care of us for the rest of our days?"

With confusion, I stared at her. "I'm a psychic. Not a witch, a priest, or an author who can write those into existence. Do you even know what psychics do?"

She nodded, "Just wishful thinking, I guess."

Wistfully, I answered, "I could go for a sexy vampire daddy though."

In unison, we sighed.

After a moment, I said, "Since I have no intention of taking another midnight walk to the cemetery, I believe we need to do a salt circle."

"Like they did in Hocus Pocus?" she asked.

"Yes! Exactly. In my experience, it should prevent any spirits from crossing the boundary of the room."

Alice glanced around the room and shook her head. "We may have underestimated the size of the room and the amount of salt we have. We may not have enough."

With a glance around, I nodded in agreement. "I had wanted to do the bathroom, bed, windows, and perimeter, but I don't anticipate that's going to work. Maybe we can do the perimeter of the room. I have no intention of taking a moonlight stroll to that cemetery again."

"Regardless, you're going to get charged a cleaning fee," Alice replied.

"Do you have a vacuum I could borrow before I leave?"

"Yeah…," she nodded slowly. "Or you could ask the front desk for theirs."

"I'll make sure to clean it up."

As carefully as possible, we created a thin line of salt as close to the wall as we could, both to keep the mess hidden from housekeeping and to preserve our salt supply. This wouldn't be a permanent fix, but I could ensure at night I wasn't going to be whisked off on another midnight walk. The line would need to be checked daily to make sure it was still intact.

"Will this prevent Bradley from getting back in?"

"Yes, but I don't think he's coming back," I said.

"Why?" Alice gasped.

"After seeing those spirits earlier today, I think that Bradley was called by whatever was calling them," I answered.

"Shouldn't we go and find him? Obviously, not right now. It's dark and that is a bad idea to go into a haunted cemetery at night," she replied.

"Going in there unprepared could get us killed. We have no

idea what's in there. The spirits in there aren't acting normal. I'm not ready to be a ghost yet either."

Alice nodded in agreement. She placed the crystals around the room. I sprinkled a little bit of the holy water around the room and chanted, "To the windows, to the walls…That feels wrong…"

"Why won't you come with me and stay at my parents' house? I'm sure Hazel or Piper would be happy to have you stay with them too. It's foolish to stay here," Alice pleaded.

"It doesn't feel safe because it isn't. But Bradley is missing and something deep in my soul is telling me that I need to stay. Nothing in my life makes sense right now. I'm a TV psychic, D list celebrity, hiding from my agent and personal assistant. I've picked up both a hitchhiking ghost and a group of extraordinarily fun people, saved a girl from hypothermia in the woods, and am being actively possessed and manipulated by a cemetery full of ghosts. Most of that is not normal."

Alice, without saying anything, walked to me and hugged me tightly. The moment her warm arms wrapped around me, I clung to her like Violet had clung to me in the woods.

Just because I was determined to stay and not run from whatever danger was ahead of me, didn't mean I wasn't terrified.

"I have a crazy idea. Let's have a sleepover!" Alice exclaimed.

"That seems reckless. What if they try to take you too?" I stated matter of factly.

"It doesn't seem to want me. Remember, I had no problem driving us earlier today." Then she snapped her fingers and asked, "What if I get the group here? Safety in numbers!"

I sighed. "What can I do to get you to leave?"

She hugged me again. "There's nothing you can do. You're

stuck with me," she announced as she began to text on her phone. Moments later, my phone chimed.

Alice: Quest alert! Cassandra needs round-the-clock protection. Weird things are happening over here at the motel. Will you answer the call to protect the village psychic from unknown peril? If so, Zander, please gather your party and arrive with much haste to room 1007. Parking is limited so carpooling is appreciated. Prepare and gather your supplies for a few nights. What say you?

Zander: I hear the call and respond with an overwhelming hell yes! I'll do the usual rounds. Leaving here in T minus one hour.

Hazel: I'm already ready.

Piper: Get me last.

Zander: I always do.

Bear: I'll be ready in ten. Mom made dinner if you want to grab a plate while you're here.

Zander: Yes! Be there in fifteen.

Alice: Oh! And everyone bring some salt.

Bear: I get the sense that you're not telling us everything...

Hazel: It's already packed.

Piper: Zander, grab your moms extra saltshaker for me.

Zander: Will do.

"My room isn't big enough for six of us," I stated. "And I'm not sleeping on the floor."

Alice headed to the window and pulled the curtain back to see out to the side. "There's not a car parked next door."

"Ok," I said slowly.

"My assumption is that it's not rented for the night. Your room has an adjoining door. We can rent it and throw the door open for the most epic sleepover."

Before I could reply, she was out the door. I watched her run straight to the front office. Within moments, she was back, face shining and a large plastic keychain in her hand. Then she texted the group.

Alice: Slight change of location. Room 1006 has been held for the party. Headquarters will be in 1007.

An hour and a half later, Zander's van pulled up and the group tumbled out with arms loaded. Sleeping bags, pillows, coolers, zippered bags, and grocery bags overflowed with food. So commenced the first sleepover I had since I was a kid. Hopefully, no one would freeze our bras or put anyone's hands in warm water.

Ten

Dear Johnny

As soon as Zander, Piper, Hazel, and Bear were in their room, they threw open their side of the adjoining room door and began banging. "Open up! The party has arrived!"

Alice quickly unlocked and opened our side. She jumped up and down in excitement. "This is going to be phenomenal!"

Piper, who wore a pair of neon mushroom pajamas, stepped over the thin white line of salt. With a manicured finger, she pointed instantly at it. "That's an odd way to store your cocaine. Generally, it's not recommended to use it that way."

Zander, who wore a red plaid pair of pajamas, rested his head on her shoulder and said, "Gotta be careful when snorting off the floor. It's not sanitary. And can you imagine if there's a stray staple or fingernail clipping mixed in?" He pinched his nose.

My head dropped into my hands and I hissed, "It's not

cocaine. Can you please stop saying that word? Someone will hear, and we'll get kicked out. It's salt. Plain, ol' iodized salt."

Bear, quiet as always in a black pair of pajama pants and T-shirt, positioned himself to stand next to Alice. Hazel, in a pink lacy floor length nightgown, complete with matching silk robe and high heeled shoes, approached me and hugged me gently.

Piper shrugged and said, "In honor of a sleepover, we have all the things that we used to sneak into our sleepovers when we were teens."

Bear replied, "Beer being the most important."

Hazel added, "And wine!"

Zander added, "And I brought my tarot cards and Ouija board. With being so close to that creepy cemetery, this place is crawling with ghosts. They're almost tangible!"

I shook my head and asked, "You know about the cemetery?"

Zander's eyes grew wide with excitement. "Of course I do! Our local ghost hunting investigators were on my podcast a few years ago. They told me all about the ghosts that reside there." He smiled widely and added, "You've felt the ghosts, haven't you?"

"Yes, I have. But not here. They're all in the cemetery," I said.

"I highly doubt that. Anyway, I can't wait to set this stuff up," he prattled on as he pulled out the Ouija board.

Alice stood next to me and said, "Cassandra can already speak to the dead. Why do we need to use that?"

"Besides, I'm of the mindset that Ouija boards don't work through honest spirit manipulation," I added.

Zander smiled wickedly, "So it's all just a bunch of hocus pocus."

I didn't like his smile and knew that if we tried to use the Ouija board he had something planned. It was written plain across his face.

"This is a foolish idea thought up by a foolish young man," I replied.

Zander scowled for a moment before he nodded and said, "It's your loss." He turned toward the dresser to set the Ouija board down. From over his shoulder he added, "But there's something strange at the cemetery that calls you, right?"

Disappointed, I pursed my lips as I looked at Alice and said, "You told them."

She shrugged. "Well, yeah. They needed to know what was going on. You're not alone in this."

Around the group I saw them all nod in agreement. "We're here to help," Hazel replied.

Zander turned around, his wicked smile back, a sealed Ouija board box still in his hands. "No better time than the present. I got us a brand-new board so as not to bring any new energy into this space."

My mouth hung open as each member of the group nodded reluctantly. He walked up to me and whispered, "It's not like I'm suggesting that we use it in the cemetery. That's something someone stupid would do in a horror movie. I'd like to make it home tomorrow in one piece."

Piper zipped into the adjoining room and brought back a small box with the word Tarot printed on the side. She grabbed the Ouija board box from Zander and sat down on the floor. Hazel sat next to her and the pair got to opening the boxes. Bear and Zander glanced at each other for a second before sitting on either side of them. Alice pulled on my hand and brought me to the circle. Bear patted the floor beside him. She smiled at him warmly and went to sit.

In the center of our group was the Ouija board, pristine with its shiny sticker front reflecting the light above us.

Hazel jumped up and ran to her room. Moments later, she brought back a bag of LED candles. She tossed one to each of us. Then she turned off the lights in the room.

Once she rejoined the group and the candles glowed softly beside us, she announced, "Much better!"

Silence and nerves grew between us. There was no way I would be the first to put my fingertips on the planchette. It wasn't that I believed that any manufactured Ouija board held any powers, but I was still nervous. My sisters and I had grown up using one. The only time it "worked" was when someone in the group was trying to deceive the others by moving it themselves.

"Let's put our fingers on it together," Piper instructed.

Alice nodded. "On the count of three. One. Two…"

Zander interrupted her by placing his finger on the plastic planchette and then added, "Three."

Quickly, everyone else placed one of their fingers beside Zander's. Almost immediately, the planchette began to move around the board in large sweeping circles.

Then it began to hover over letters. Out loud, we repeated what it was spelling.

"My name is Agustus. I died here 100 years ago."

Alice shivered and Bear wrapped a protective arm around her. "It's ok."

The planchette moved again. "Someone must die tonight so my soul can rest."

I searched the faces around the group, disappointed that I had been correct. It had only taken someone a few seconds before they manipulated the board. There wasn't a hint of a spirit in the room. The salt had made sure of that.

Bear, Alice, and Hazel all stared at the planchette, wide-eyed and unblinking.

The excitement that radiated from Zander and Piper was hard to miss.

Two can play this game, I thought to myself. With a subtle force, I guided the planchette and carefully watched them for clues to who the culprit was. Neither of their faces changed as the planchette zigzagged across the board.

With only a gut instinct, I took a guess.

The group repeated the words I spelled.

"Zander. You are chosen."

In shock, his fingers jumped away from the board. As soon as his contact was broken, the planchette refused to move under the fingers of the remaining group and the "spirits" were quiet again.

"They're joking, right?" Zander shouted, his voice shaky with panic. "Who did that? One of you moved it. Who did it?"

Piper hugged Zander. "It's just a silly board game."

"Only someone truly duplicitous would do something to make the group believe the spirits were talking, when they truly weren't," I stated sharply as I locked eyes with him. It was years of frauds that gave psychics the name charlatan, and I didn't take that lightly.

Alice glanced between me and Zander.

"You were moving the planchette, weren't you?" she asked him.

"No. That's stupid. This is stupid," he answered and pushed the planchette across the board. He got up and left the room.

Piper got up and retrieved the box. "I don't want to play with this anymore," she said. As her fingers brushed the planchette, everyone's eyes watched in anticipation for the spirit to return to give us more information. "Do you think Zander is in danger?"

I shook my head and answered, "No. The only spirit we made contact with tonight was the spirit of a jokester. Zander is safe."

Quickly, Piper put the board away and threw it on the bed. She then followed Zander into the room next door.

I nodded at them. "Something going on between them?"

Hazel shrugged. "When they're on the same page, it's either divine or diabolical."

Alice met my eyes. "Did you move the planchette?"

"Only the last part when I named Zander as the sacrifice. I couldn't tell if it was Zander or Piper moving it but knew it was one of them. I made an educated guess. I assume I got it correct," I said.

Alice sighed heavily and nodded. "I was hoping we had contacted a spirit. It seems everything 'haunted' here in the Dells is only for tourists and is always exaggerated."

Bear side hugged her and then asked, "Do you know how to read tarot?"

Alice and Hazel shook their heads. "Zander is the one who usually reads for us," Hazel added.

Slowly, I rolled my eyes and asked, "Does he act like this a lot?"

Bear nodded. "He tries to convince us that he has all these *amazing* abilities. Don't get me wrong, he's a superb Dungeon Master. His imagination is impressive…" he said and then trailed off.

"He's a phenomenal DM," Hazel piped up. "He's just a…" She

too trailed off.

Alice picked up where Hazel left off, "He's prickly when it comes to pranks being pulled on him."

"Gotcha. So, he can trick you, but he can't take a joke himself," I replied.

"That's unfortunately true," Bear said.

"If he's your primary tarot reader, I'm guessing he's as unreliable with his readings as with the Ouija board," I added.

Hazel nodded and said, "He once told me my grandma was going to die in the near future." In a whisper she added, "That was three years ago, and she is a member of a senior only tap-dancing group. I mean, she's old, so I know she won't live forever, but it made me incredibly anxious for a long time after that."

I dropped my head in my hands and said, "Please don't tell me he gets paid for any of this. Tell me this is his schtick at parties and get-togethers."

Alice blushed, "No. He believes that he's an empath and truly in tune with the spirit world."

I pushed myself off the floor and realized I hadn't been on the floor for an exceedingly long time. Getting up was harder than it used to be. My mother's words of 'Just wait until you're forty and the floor is no longer your friend,' played in my ears. Luckily, I still had two more years until then, but I made a mental note to start working on getting up and down off the floor more.

Quickly, I passed the worn box on the bed and opened my dresser instead. In the far back was a box that I tended to bring with me. Even in a rush, it was always added to my trip. There have been times when I don't remember packing it but find it with my possessions.

It was a small blue, plaid, hinged plastic box, with a handle and lock. Luckily, when I lost the key years ago, the box hadn't been locked.

I returned to the group and sat with my legs crossed.

The candlelight played over the box.

The hinge creaked as I opened it and the three leaned over to see inside.

Wrapped in black satin, were three decks of tarot cards.

The first was the set I had purchased as a teenager from an out of business chain bookstore. It wasn't a set I felt any spiritual connection to, beyond the nostalgia that it had been the first deck of tarot cards I had held. Through sentiment alone, I would never get rid of the deck.

The second was a set I was gifted by my parents for my twenty-first birthday— an Arthurian legend deck that guided me through my twenties with fair reliability. At the time, I had been fascinated by King Arthur, which helped me remember the meanings of the cards. The illustrations match the story with the meaning of each card, so if you know the story on the card, you can begin to figure out what the card means.

The third, my favorite, had since given me the most accuracy and the most connection I had ever felt from a deck. A Last Unicorn deck, gold foiled and elegant. My aunt Kathy, from my mother's side, had gone shopping with me at a local used bookstore. She had a penchant for the paranormal and strange. The moment she walked into the store she was drawn to the collection of tarot cards behind the counter. When she saw my excitement at finding a Last Unicorn deck, she had informed the clerk to ring it up.

The trio sat around, hands itching to touch and explore, but unsure of the "rules." I nodded at them and said, "You can pick them up. They're all special to me, and I trust you to treat them with care."

Each of them chose a deck and contemplated the artwork on the cards.

Bear, with my first deck, stated, "You're more generous than Zander. He never lets us touch his cards."

"Every tarot card reader has their own rules and preferences. I don't believe there are any right or wrong, only what works for the reader," I replied. However, internally, I suspected that Zander was using his rules to make it seem as if he held more knowledge and power than he in truth possessed.

"What do we want to find out?" Hazel asked the group.

Alice, with the Arthurian Legends deck in hand, answered, "Let's start with finding out where Bradley is." When she saw the confusion on Hazel and Bear's faces, she added, "He's Cassandra's hitchhiker ghost. She picked him up in Beloit."

They nodded as if this was a normal statement and it made me realize how much I liked them.

A light knock on the door interrupted my thoughts and when we glanced up, Piper was standing there. Her head was lowered and her eyes were red from crying.

"I knew what Zander was planning. But when his name came up on the board, I thought we had contacted a spirit. Maybe Zander was more intuitive than I had thought," she said softly. "When I went over to talk to him, he was mad. Ranted about you, Cassandra. Said he thought you were a fraud and were actively trying to steal his friends. I told him I didn't think that was true."

Alice gasped in disgust. "We have more than enough space for all of our friends."

Piper nodded. "I told him as much, but he wouldn't listen.

He said that Cassandra was over here poisoning you against him." She hung her head before continuing. "Then, he said that I was the only true friend he had. He asked me to do something I couldn't do."

Bear crossed his arms and asked, "What did he ask?"

Piper replied, "He asked me to choose. Him or you all. I couldn't abandon you all. You've been there with me for years. I asked him to reconsider, but he said I had made my choice. He grabbed his stuff and left."

In moments, she was wrapped in a group hug.

"We're going to do some tarot cards with Cassandra. Want to see one of her decks?" Alice asked as she guided Piper back to our circle.

In the simplest tarot spread I could remember off the top of my head, I laid out three cards next to each other in a row.

I reached for the first and flipped it. "The first, to show the past." The Death card. Gasps surrounded me. "Don't worry. Rarely does this actually mean death. But in this case, it could mean Bradley's beginning. This card usually means a type of transition or the end of something."

Alice laughed nervously, "He's already dead so his transition from alive to ghost."

I nodded. "Could be."

The second card, The Fool. "This is the present."

Hazel inspected the card and said, "The name doesn't seem like it's a flattering card."

"It means adventure. Additionally, it could indicate a leap into the unknown," I replied.

Alice glanced at me and replied, "Like how you threw yourself into a road trip with no planning and how you… acquired Bradley?"

I nodded a little. That was exactly what I had thought.

The third card, Seven of Swords. "This is the future or what is to come," I announced.

Bear leaned closer and examined the card. "I don't believe that means Bradley is simply sunbathing somewhere."

With a shake of my head, I replied, "No. It doesn't. It means someone is being sneaky or secretive. Unfortunately, I don't believe that Bradley left of his own free will. Something is behind his disappearance, but this isn't giving us any insight into who took him."

"So, unless we wander into that cemetery, you may never get Bradley back?" Alice asked.

"Seems about right," I replied sullenly.

Alice yawned and Bear checked the time on his phone. "It's late. Let's get some sleep."

Everyone nodded in agreement. Quickly, I wrapped the decks in the satin and placed them into the box. When the box was safely put into the drawer again, I bid goodnight to everyone.

The three friends retreated back to their room while Alice stayed with me. "You can go back over there if you want," I told her.

"Nah. I can't have you whisked off into the night," she replied as she got into bed. "Besides, we need to finish planning the viewing party for your show!"

"Do we honestly need to do that now? Everyone knows where I'm at now," I whined.

"Yes. It's in your best interest."

Eleven

King Of Wishful Thinking

"Planning for the viewing party," translated to shopping for clothes with Alice, Hazel, and Piper. The three of them used me as a doll to dress up. The viewing party was that night, and it was already noon. So far, nothing I had been forced into was a viable option, in my opinion.

From the dressing room, I pulled yet another dress over my head and whined to the group, "I *do* have clothes that I brought. I could wear them instead."

Boos and hisses were their only response.

When I opened the door to show off the pink and purple atrocity they forced me to try on, I was met with tilted heads and their thumbs down.

"You know that fast fashion is an environmental problem, right?" I asked the group while holding the dress out in my hands. "This is hurting our environment."

Under her breath, Piper added, "And our eyes."

Hazel snapped her fingers, "If fast fashion is what is holding you back, I have an idea. To the thrift store!" I barely had time to change before they were dragging me to another store to find vintage threads.

I expected to find musty smelling, granny clothes being run by a group of volunteers. Instead, we stepped into an adorable consignment boutique. Transformed from an old farmhouse, it now used the rooms as gallery spaces. Dresses, coats, and shoes in what I assumed was an old dining room. The old living room held pants, tops, handbags, and other accessories.

Local artists and crafts people had their wares displayed throughout the shop.

Everyone spread out and began choosing pieces for me. Instantly, I was attracted to vintage t-shirts and a pair of black, chunky heeled boots. Before anyone could stop me, I grabbed a Green Day T-shirt, the boots, and a red flannel shirt and ran to the dressing room.

As I changed, I could hear my friends calling for me. When they asked one of the employees, she replied, "She's trying on clothes."

Outside the dressing room, they waited for me. The moment they saw my outfit, their faces fell in disappointment, and I knew I had chosen the right outfit.

"This is what I'm comfortable with. If I have to race around to different bars tonight, I need to be able to move. No dresses or skirts with high heeled shoes," I announced.

Hazel and Piper each hid a pair of high heels behind their backs. Alice nonchalantly put a handful of flowy dresses back onto a nearby rack.

Piper held up one hand and said, "You win. Wear what you want, even if it screams 1994."

With a wide smile, I replied, "They say to embrace what makes you happy, and this makes me happy. I feel youthful in this, like I did as a kid."

"At least let us help you pick out some accessories," Hazel said as she reached for a shoulder bag with black ruffles and silver accents along the ridges. She held it up by its chain linked handle.

Piper squealed and ran to the necklace rack. Quickly, she came back with a silver chain with a red garnet cut into a star pendant. "This. You *need* this."

Then Alice, silent as a ghost, reappeared when I hadn't even noticed her wander off. In her hands she held up a black miniskirt with a tiny slit up one leg.

Of course, it was the perfect size and fit me better than I could have guessed.

After changing back into my clothes, we took my purchases to the counter. Each of us had a handful of items and I was surrounded by laughter and chitchat. In that instant, I wanted to pull them all into me and give them a hug.

For the first time in a long time, I was included in a friend group. A friend group of girls. No one was calling me a freak. No one was calling me weird or asking where my warts were. These young women knew about my abilities and found me compelling enough to hang out with.

As we left the boutique, I said, "Thank you for shopping with me and making me buy something. I don't have anyone to go shopping with besides my mom. Usually, I go by myself and buy only things that are necessary."

Hazel replied immediately, "All of these things were necessary. Especially everything I bought myself." She held up a large bag that was filled to the top.

We all laughed and walked side by side to my car.

As we drove back to the motel, Alice asked, "Cassandra, is there anyone special back home you've got your eyes on?"

I barked a laugh. "No. Absolutely not. The most action I've gotten this year is from that seagull stealing my bikini."

Piper met my eyes in the rearview mirror and asked, "No cute ex-boyfriend longing for another chance?"

I almost vomited in my mouth. "There is an ex-boyfriend, Zack. Thankfully, I haven't heard from him for months. He's a troll."

Hazel lifted her fingers to her temples and shut her eyes. "I'm sensing some hot tea here."

I laughed and replied, "The 'hot tea' is that he used me for my money for years." Then in a quieter voice, I felt compelled to share details no one else in the world knew. "He told me that I was lucky to have him because who else could love someone like me."

Horrified gasps erupted from each of the women. "He did *not*!" Alice yelled. "You are a delight."

I laughed nervously as I was on a slippery slope with the other secrets I held deep inside me. Things that I was ashamed that Zack had told me over the years that I believed.

Alice caught my eye and a look of concern crossed her face. I sensed she could tell there were things I wasn't saying. She softly said, "Sometimes, when we don't have anyone to talk to, we end up in situations that we regret. The important thing is to get it out, when you're ready, and tell others what happened. There's no shame here. We're all women, and I think all of us have had horrid boyfriends before."

Nods and noises of agreement sounded around the car.

Piper and Hazel's hands rested on my shoulders from behind

me. "I'm sure your soulmate is out there somewhere," Hazel said wistfully. "You simply haven't met them yet."

"It's not Bradley, for sure," I laughed. With a smile, I shook my head and continued to drive. The desire to get the attention off of me and my failed relationship was too much, and I asked a question that I had been wanting to ask for days. "Alice, what's up with you and Bear? He's at work right now, so we can talk freely."

Her mouth dropped open and she shrugged. "What about B…Bear?," she asked as her voice caught on his name.

Giggles from Piper and Hazel erupted from the back seat. "She doesn't recognize that he adores her," Piper laughed. "Alice always tells us we're seeing things that aren't there."

"Alice, please tell me you *see* the way he looks and acts around you. He wraps you in his arms and purposely stands next to you," I stated with no humor in my voice.

Her face turned a deep red, and she shook her head. "You're imagining things, exactly like those two," she replied and pointed to the back seat. "He's considerate, that's all. Besides, if he liked me that way, he'd tell me."

"Maybe he believes you don't like him that way," I stated softly. "*Do* you like him that way?"

She shrugged again, "I don't know. He's Bear. Sweet, kind, handsome, Bear." Her tone had taken on a dreamy quality by the time she said his name again.

"How long have you liked him?" I asked.

With an exaggerated sigh, she answered, "Since the fifth grade when he moved here. I thought he saw me more as a sister, so I've convinced myself that it was weird that I'd like him like that."

Hazel and Piper's hands reached over to squeeze Alice's

shoulders. "I haven't known Bear very long, but I get the sense that he's waiting to get confirmation from you that you feel the same," I said softly.

Piper gasped, "Is that your psychic ability telling you that?"

With a sigh, I answered, "My common sense tells me that. Not everything I say is because I'm psychic. I have eyes."

When we arrived at the hotel, we rushed inside. Then Hazel announced, "It's time to get ready!"

With the adjoining door open, Piper played music so we could dance and sing. Their joy and assistance that afternoon felt fortifying, like they were building me up for the night ahead. Perhaps, they were rebuilding my foundation that had crumbled underneath me.

Hazel and Piper helped me with my makeup and gave me black winged eyeliner. I had never successfully recreated the look myself, but they had done it effortlessly.

An hour and a half later, Piper and Hazel were ready. Hazel's flowy sage green velvet skirt with its matching bell sleeved top swirled around her as she spun for us. Around her waist was an antiqued gold belt.

The pair of tight black leather pants that Piper wore accentuated her height and build. They definitely gave Sandy from *Grease* vibes. The black top she wore had a crescent moon that was accented by a black corded choker that had tiny crescent moons dangling around it.

Alice, who had disappeared into the bathroom, came out wearing a 90's vintage floral print dress that had tiny black buttons up from hem to scoop necked collar. She had twisted her hair up into a messy bun. The chunky black boots she wore completed the ensemble.

We all clapped for her.

I said, "You're stunning! I am speechless."

"Let's get some selfies," Piper said and waved us to her. She positioned us expertly for photos that immediately were posted online. Our phones dinged as we were tagged in each social media post.

Hazel squealed and announced, "Every bar has at least fifty people interested in your event tonight!"

"The locals come out when the tourists are away," Piper said.

When I pulled my car keys out, Piper pushed my hand down. "You, my dear, will not be driving this evening. We've arranged for you to use a chauffeured car tonight." In a whispered hush, she leaned over and informed me, "It's Hazel's little brother in their parents car, but his rate was reasonable and we promised to give him a five-star rating online."

Outside, the sun had sunk below the horizon. Reds and oranges were cast onto the sky. In the parking lot, Hazel's brother, Ellis, stood patiently by a minivan. He was a tall, teddy bear of a guy who towered over the vehicle. The navy-blue suit he wore fit him perfectly. He flashed his gorgeous smile and opened the van door for us. After we were inside, he shut the door.

"Alright, ladies, I'm your designated driver tonight. Hazel gave me the itinerary for the evening, and I will get you there safely," he announced.

"Thank you, Ellis," I said.

We took more selfies and posted on social media as we drove to the first location, The Moose Bar and Grill. Large wooden carved moose sculptures lined the sidewalk that had moose prints leading to the restaurant. Inside, a large, mounted moose head hung over the entrance. Immediately, the smell of fried food wafted in the air. The room buzzed with chatter.

Around the walls, hung large screen TVs, all of them on the *Echo* streaming service, watching last week's episode of *The Emberford Psychic*. On the bar, a large countdown timer was on. Two hours and five minutes until my new episode aired.

Cheers around the room came as I was recognized by fans of the show. I smiled nervously and waved.

At the center of it all, stood Bear, and his eyes lasered in on Alice. He gulped visibly, and I gave him a thumbs up. Piper and I pushed her toward him and whispered, "Go."

We watched as if we were extras in the background of their rom-com movie friends to lovers moment. After they exchanged a few words, Bear led her outside. Piper, Hazel, and I snuck over to a nearby window in time to see Bear wrap Alice in his arms and pull her in for a kiss.

Softly, their lips touched, tentative and shy. Her eyes fluttered closed. I pulled the collars of Hazel and Piper and nodded to the rest of the room. "Let's give them some space," I said.

In unison, with disappointment they replied, "Aww."

Once they were away from the window, they began to mingle around the room. People came up for autographs and simply to say hello. Instantly, I knew that I would never remember the names or faces of so many people. And there were still a few bars to make an appearance at. How on earth was I going to survive the night?

When I felt a tap on my shoulder, I turned to see a middle-aged couple holding hands with a little girl that I would have recognized anywhere.

Violet Chandler.

Twelve

Aces & Eights

The woman let go of Violet and threw her arms around me. "Thank you for saving my little girl," she sobbed. The man shifted uncomfortably behind her, but within moments tears began to well in his own eyes. Soon, he too wrapped his arms around us. Both sobbed a thank you into my shoulders.

Around the room, eyes watched and waited to see how I would react and handle the situation. Phones were out and up, taking in our interaction. The judgment was weighing more than the couple's combined pressure on my shoulders.

As I gently patted each of their backs, something caught my attention. Something hovered over Violet. A shimmery hazy cloud that was barely visible to me. All the suspicions I had about how easily I had found Violet were clear instantly. Violet wasn't alone, now or when she had been in the woods. Someone close to the family had watched over her.

"I'm so glad I could help," I whispered, a lump in my throat.

They clung to me for a few moments longer and then the man let go. When the woman continued to hug me tightly, the man cleared his throat. The woman nodded and detangled herself from me.

"I'm so sorry, I didn't even introduce myself. I'm Charlotte Chandler," she said with a rich Minnesota accent. She reached over to a napkin dispenser and grabbed a handful of them. Then, she began to wipe her face, but the tears continued to fall. Her gray eyes matched a streak of gray in her light brown braid.

The man held out his hand and introduced himself, "Name's Matthew Chandler." He was tall with a full head of skin. Like his wife, his blue eyes continued to brim with tears. "If she had been out there much longer, the doctors say she might not have made it."

"Right place, right time, I guess," I replied softly, but my eyes drifted back to Violet and the cloud. "I suspect that Violet has a little guardian angel watching over her, though."

Charlotte instantly said, "You're her guardian angel."

Gently, I shook my head. "Violet has someone exceptional with her at all times. I was simply the person that could help."

The couple gaped at each other, and I witnessed a wordless conversation between them. They silently stared at each other for a full minute before slowly turning back to me with a question on their faces. I didn't need to be a psychic to know that they had lost someone, probably a parent. Most likely, they had experienced some small paranormal event in their home, and it had unnerved them. But if they could believe that it was a loved one who had passed, it could ease their anxiety. What was better than the belief that someone watched over their child? Who wouldn't want that?

Before either of them could speak, I said, "Whatever is happening at home is from someone who deeply cares and loves Violet. You can talk to them. They can hear you."

The parents' shocked wide eyes told me I had been correct.

I spoke directly to the cloud, "They're going to do better to try not to scare you. I believe they were trying to let you know that they were still there watching over your family."

Charlotte instantly turned around to watch Violet as tears streaked down her face again. Matthew, however, met my eyes. "Charlotte's mom, Hannah, died before Violet was born and never got to meet her. Is it truly her?"

I nodded. "She's not talking to me, but she's watchful of Violet. At this moment, I believe that Hannah guided me to your daughter. I was unaware of her involvement before, but I don't have any doubts. Spirits will do that sometimes. They don't want or need the recognition. They could fear being sent to the light before they're ready. So, instead she guided me around that wooded lot and led me to Violet."

Matthew swallowed hard and sighed. "Thank you. We came here to thank you for helping Violet. Instead, you gave us another comfort. We're in your debt."

I smiled softly and patted him on the shoulder. "I'm so glad I came to the Dells. Glad that I was so close to her that I could help." The thought of coincidence and fate rattled around my brain. It felt like everything was connected. Every event from my show through to being in The Dells and made finding Violet more than a coincidence. What if I hadn't decided to go to Wisconsin? What if I had never met Bradley? I never would have come to The Dells, nor met Alice. I never would have been near that wooded lot. Who else would have heard

Violet's call? A shiver ran through my body.

With a nod, Matthew reached for Violet and Charlotte's hands and led them to a table across the room.

As soon as they were out of earshot, Alice raced up. "We don't have much time left here. They want you to say something."

"Wh…what?" I stammered. "That was *never* discussed."

Hazel sashayed up to us with a microphone in hand. "Here you go! Just say a few words and we'll head over to the next place."

With all eyes on me, I gulped down air as if I couldn't get enough. "Hi, I'm Cassandra Seer," I said softly.

From the back, someone yelled, "Talk into the microphone."

"Oops," I replied and then positioned the microphone in front of my mouth. "Thank you for coming tonight." The microphone echoed my voice. Someone behind the bar adjusted the speaker and gave me the thumbs up to continue. "I'm Cassandra Seer. In a little bit," I paused and checked the timer on the bar. "One hour and forty-five minutes to be exact, you're going to watch the new episode of *The Emberford Psychic*. I hope you enjoy it."

As soon as Hazel was within reach, I tossed the mic at her and approached the bartender. "I need a shot if I'm going to survive tonight."

"What's your poison?" she asked.

"I don't usually drink, so something that doesn't taste like poison," I replied.

She smiled and got to pouring. When she was done, she slid the drink across the bar to me. It resembled a tiny beer, with the foam on top. When she saw my confusion, she answered, "It's a buttery nipple. Many people like it. No poison here and low proof. We don't need you becoming a sloppy mess. If you ever feel like Emberford doesn't appreciate you, you'll always have a home here in the Dells."

I picked up the shot and drank it quickly. It was delicious. "Thank you." I handed her a ten-dollar bill.

Hazel, Piper, Alice, and Bear ushered me out of the bar and into Ellis' van.

"To Molly's!" Hazel announced and Ellis drove us.

Molly's was much smaller than The Moose. No fancy theming. Inside was darker with only a few TV's around the room, all showing last week's episode of *The Emberford Psychic*. The same countdown timer rested on the bar. Almost every table was occupied and every head turned as I entered.

"Do I need to make a speech here, too?" I asked Hazel.

"Just introduce yourself and say a few words. Then we'll order some food and eat. Next we head to our final bar and finish our bar crawl," she said.

A mic was pushed into my face, and I took it with my hand. "Hi, I'm Cassandra Seer, *The Emberford Psychic.*"

Applause and whistles greeted me.

"Well, thank you for that," I replied casually. Either I was getting more comfortable with this or else the shot had helped ease my nerves. Maybe both. "Who here has watched the first episode?"

Everyone clapped.

"Well, you made my night! Thank you! I hope you enjoy tonight's episode." Hazel took the mic from me and led us to a table. Appetizers and drinks were already waiting.

"Well, you've gotten more comfortable," Alice announced and handed me a mozzarella stick. Bear put his arm around her and her cheeks deepened to red.

"I'm glad to see you've talked," I said.

Hazel giggled, "I'd say that's the *last* thing they've been doing." Piper smiled and bumped Hazel with her side. "Ok, but honestly, it's about time. The moon eyes you've made at each other were so obvious."

We all nodded at them. Bear and Alice smiled the way that only brand new love can. Hopelessly. It was the most dazzling thing I had seen the entire trip so far.

Around the room, the screens all began to play the theme song for *The Emberford Psychic.* Then I was on screen. The bar reran the pilot episode.

My voice from the TV was far too nasally and obnoxious. With apprehension, I glanced around the room and searched for signs that I annoyed the viewers. I honestly couldn't understand how anyone could stand to listen to me for long. All eyes were glued to the TV, with an occasional side glance at me.

"My name is Cassandra Seer and I'm a psychic. In the small town, Emberford, Michigan, I found my purpose in helping my community. Spirits and the living alike guide me to those in my town that need my assistance to find closure. I am *The* Emberford Psychic, and I invite you to join me on my journey today."

Applause and cheers from the crowd surprised me. I pushed past the self-criticism of how I sounded or appeared on screen to catch a glimpse of what these people found entertaining or enjoyable.

The first thing I noticed was the show was lightly edited and showed real, unscripted conversations. Of course, when filming, there are people to talk to and topics to discuss. The first episode alone had several random conversations that made me laugh on screen. My neighbor, Mrs. Koch ran out every time she saw the camera crew, cross in hand, shouting that they were going to release the devil if they worked with me. The editing crew left several of her "scenes" in. They even created a montage showing the number of times she ran over wearing one of her many housecoats and slippers slapping her feet.

Piper leaned over and asked, "She's honestly your neighbor?"

"Yep. She wasn't invited to the shooting, but that didn't stop her, obviously," I laughed. The camera swept to her yard, full of crosses and flags.

Footage of the director, Will, came on, his short frame competing with her tiny stature. She wore a light blue housecoat with matching slippers, a large wooden cross gripped tightly in her hand. Her gray hair was wild as the wind practiced being her hairdresser.

"Mrs. Koch, we understand your point of view. You're allowed to have it, but we're here to follow Cassie," Will said gently.

I leaned into the screen and whispered, "Cassandra." With a slow wave, I leaned back out again.

Will turned back to me and corrected himself. "Cassandra. We'll be out of here in a few weeks. We've already adjusted our shooting hours to accommodate you. This is a done deal and we're going to finish filming. If you continue to come here, we're going to ask you to stop trespassing."

Mrs. Koch held up her hands to cover her face. "I don't give you permission to film me."

Will turned to the camera and shook his head. "Then please stop coming over here when we're filming." The cameraman turned the camera, and it cut to interviews of other townspeople talking about their loved ones who passed.

Luckily, Mrs. Koch didn't have loved ones trying to reconnect with her. Or else they were judgemental of me and my family and wouldn't associate with us.

For the remainder of the episode, I spoke with spirits and the living. In an interview, I announced, "Helping spirits doesn't always mean guiding them to the 'light.' Sometimes, it means helping the living find closure and comfort that their loved one is ok. That they haven't disappeared into nothing. We all want to know someone is watching out for us and that this life has meaning."

When the last words were uttered and the closing sound played, the bar clapped and eyes turned to me. People clamored to come over and give their impressions or stories.

"My mother passed away and a local psychic helped us. It truly made my grief so much better," one woman said as she grasped my hands.

After she was done, a man came up and whispered, "Thank you for what you do. Have you ever thought of going on a talk show and speaking with the audience?"

I shook my head but smiled sweetly. "Thanks for the suggestion. I'll keep it in mind."

When the crowd dissipated, the four of us paid our bill and left the bar to go to the final destination, Eddie's.

In the car, everyone talked at once about their favorite parts of the show.

Hazel stated, "I *cannot* imagine having that woman for a neighbor. She's insufferable."

I nodded, "Yep. She is. She wasn't supposed to be on camera, but she constantly came over to interrupt. She's disliked my family since we moved in," I said.

Piper replied, "If you ever need character witnesses to talk about how you are in real life, pick me! I'll talk about how you're very much like that in person without cameras."

"I appreciate that," I replied.

Ellis pulled up in front of the final bar. Its bright lights in the parking lot broke through the growing darkness and haziness of the night.

We got out of the car and headed inside. The room was packed and we heard the opening lines from *The Emberford Psychic* again. Eyes turned to me and applause greeted us.

"Cassie!" someone shouted from the bar His voice carried above the others.

I didn't even need to see who it was. His voice was recognizable in any situation.

It was Jack, my agent. His shaved hair couldn't disguise the horseshoe ring around his head. He wore a black jacket and dark blue jeans. With a beer in hand, he approached with a wide, toothy smile.

"You didn't think I would find out about this? Let you do this all on your own? Take all the credit for this, did you?" he asked loudly.

"Actually, I had hoped that we wouldn't be talking again," I said, matter of factly. "You threatened me."

He scanned the space around him and finally noticed that the people around us were openly eavesdropping. Quickly, Jack took a deep drink from his pint before he replied quietly, "Cassie. Threaten is such an ugly word. Everything I've done, I've done for you. My intentions were pure. I only want your success." He winked at me and took another drink. "You could thank me. Without my interference, you *never* would have come here. You were smart to document your little vacation with your fans. And the stunt of rescuing that little girl? Chef's kiss." He brought his fingers to his mouth and kissed them.

"Let's circle back to what you did," I demanded.

He shook his head. "If I tell you, I know that you'll get mad at me and won't see it for the labor of love that it is."

"You tell yourself that to make whatever you've done seem better. What did you do?" I asked again.

He took another drink, turned away from me, and refused to answer. But a thought repeated in my mind, a rising suspicion that I hadn't allowed myself to seriously consider or believe. With him in front of me, I had my chance to try my theory out with the best chance to be able to spot the lie. He would most likely deny what I was going to say, but with any luck, he wouldn't expect me to guess.

"You told the tabloid where I was going to be that day at the beach," I stated.

"What makes you say that?" he asked but refused to meet my eyes.

"It's the truth. Laverna had my location and you took advantage of that fact. You leaked it and then benefited from it by cultivating interviews," I replied.

A biker nearby elbowed his friend and the two walked closer to Jack, their arms crossed and scowls on their faces.

Jack shook his head at the pair and moved me closer to a corner. In one final gulp, he finished his beer. With a hiss, he said, "Sounds to me you're listening a bit too closely to conspiracy theories."

I shook my head, "Jack. I'm not going to entertain you any further. You're fired."

"Your show is doomed to fail without me. No one wanted the show. I'm the one who sold you to them. You were a failed boring person in a nothing town," he snapped. "If you fire me,

I'll make sure they know how fake you genuinely are."

"Seems to me, with the help of people who truly care about me, my show is doing just fine," I snapped.

Before he could reply, from over his shoulder, I heard someone whisper a name. With squared shoulders, I planted myself in front of Jack and asked, "Who is Jason?" With watchful eyes, I searched for recognition on his face.

"I have no idea who that is," he replied defensively. His eyes rolled and I wasn't sure if he was lying.

"Jason tells me that is a lie," I stated and began taking slow steps toward him. "This may be the first time you're hearing his name spoken to you, you *know* his name."

When I glanced to my left and right, my friends held their phones up in front of their faces, bright lights shining as they recorded him.

"You're crazy," he said as he backed away.

"What did you do to Jason?" I asked again and took a few steps closer. "What did you do to him?"

"I don't know any Jason's," he announced again. He shook his head and avoided my eyes. He was lying.

"Jason Freelander. He is telling me otherwise," I said and then leaned toward Jack and listened. After a moment, I continued. "Mmm. That sounds awful, Jason. I can't believe he would do something like that." I paused and placed my forefinger to my lips and added, "Actually, I can."

Jack scanned left and right before he shrugged. "I honestly don't know who or what you're talking about." An almost imperceptible twitch of his eye told me he knew exactly who I was talking about.

I tapped my forefinger against my lips and listened again. "Oh, I see. Jack ran you off the road five years ago and you're still a missing person."

That's when Jack's eyes widened and his hands came out toward me. "You are lying," he shrieked.

Phones pressed closer, their bright lights blinding. "You didn't bother calling the police. Instead, you stood on the side of the road and watched his car sink into the river. Once you were sure he didn't survive and all evidence of his car was underwater, you drove away. Every once in a while you would check to see if any cars were found and were relieved every single time to find nothing. You didn't know his name when he died but learned it when you saw a missing person flyer with the make and model of his car. You've dreaded this moment every day for five years."

His face drained and had taken on a bilious olive hue.

"You're going to end our working relationship and if I were you, I would turn myself in before any more time has passed. If this crowd is any indication, these videos are going to go viral," I whispered in his ear.

Jack lifted a fist as if to punch me, but Bear appeared out of nowhere and tapped him on the shoulder. Slowly, Jack lowered his fist and gulped. "I don't need you! You can't fire me, *Cassie*. I quit!"

He turned and fled the bar.

As soon as he was out of sight, I texted Laverna. "Thank you for your service, but effective immediately, Jack Kress is no longer in my employment. Since he is the person that arranges your salary, I believe your employment is tied to his."

She didn't respond, but I could tell she had read the text. A tiny read receipt showed under my message. I shrugged and felt a weight lift off my shoulders.

The transparent spirit of Jason Freelander appeared and

smiled at me. He began to wave his farewell and turned toward the door to follow Jack.

"Wait!" I called.

He turned slowly and he smiled again.

All eyes were on me, despite the TVs around the room airing the new episode of *The Emberford Psychic*. Why would anyone watch something that was pre-recorded when there was real life drama right in front of them? Imagine the gossip that would ensue because of this interaction.

I waved and left the bar with Jason behind me.

When we were alone, I said, "Thank you for helping me with Jack. How are you here with him though? Are you haunting him?"

Jason shifted from leg to leg before answering. For the first time, I heard him speak not in a whisper. His voice was high and soft, like that of a teenager. "Yeah. I've been haunting since the day I died. Been following him around for years."

"I had no idea what he had done to you. I'm surprised you never let me know you were around," I said.

He laughed nervously. "I wasn't sure if you were trustworthy. You were working with Jack. Guilty by association."

"I never would have hired him if I had known. I'm sorry."

He shrugged. "It's ok."

"The authorities are going to find you soon. You and your family will finally have closure. There's no need to haunt Jack any longer. Is there anything you need from me before you go?"

"No, I don't believe so. Once they find me, I know I can leave. But you have something that you need to ask though, don't you?"

I nodded, "Yes. You're not from here, but I need some

help. I've noticed that most of the spirits here are in a certain cemetery. Despite how many spirits there, they won't approach me, which isn't something I'm used to."

Jason nodded, "You're attractive to us spirits. You kinda… glow."

"A friend of mine told me that recently. Do you know what's inside that cemetery? Or what they're wanting?" I asked.

"I don't. I feel the pull though. If I was going to be here longer, I don't know how long I would be able to resist the song," Jason replied.

"Song?"

"There's an echo of music on the wind. Barely audible, but always there. I don't know who is making the music, where it's coming from or why they want us. While it's enticing to follow it, there's something sinister beneath that makes me not want to obey their call," Jason said and slowly added, "This place is strange. The spirits that are here aren't swarming you because it's almost like you have a target on you. If they get near you, they could be caught. It's taking all their energy to avoid both you and whatever calls them."

"That makes sense. I assume that the place they want the spirits to go is the cemetery near my motel. It's overrun with ghosts. Hundreds more than what were there even a few days ago. Whoever is calling the spirits is trying to get me to go there as well," I replied.

"The older spirits that would protect this place aren't where they should be. Whether they've been taken, hiding, or have been sent onward, I don't know. Maybe I can help you. Would you like me to stay with you? I would need a ride home, though," he said.

"Of course. Where is home?," I asked.

"Fallasburg, Michigan."

"You can carpool with me and my ghost, Bradley, if I ever find him again," I replied. "My ghost friend is missing, and he's been ghostnapped."

"Let's find Bradley and get me home!" he said, his voice cracking a bit.

Thirteen

That's All I've Got To Say

Ellis drove us back to the motel. Jason, unbeknownst to the others, had squeezed in. I hadn't informed the group that I had picked up another ghost, but that felt like a conversation to have in the privacy of the room. Certainly, it was not a discussion to have in the car with Ellis. I didn't need him crashing the car. Being on the news once a trip was more than enough for me. A headline came to the front of my mind: *Emberford Psychic:* Fraud? How many "accidents" can she not see coming?

Hazel tapped on her phone and announced, "Ellis, you were a remarkable chauffeur tonight. I've given you all the stars and I've sent you money in the app."

Piper, Bear, and Alice tapped on their phones as well.

"You've got three more five-star ratings, Ellis," Hazel said with a soft smile. "Before you know it, you're going to be a top transportation company in The Dells."

Soon, we were dropped off and said good-bye to Ellis. "Thank you again for driving us everywhere tonight," I told him. As soon as he drove away, I turned to the group and announced, "We need to talk."

Once we were inside, I turned to speak to my friends.

From outside the room, Jason whispered, "Hey, can you let me in." The thin line of salt was still intact and prevented him from entering. I broke the line with my finger which allowed him to enter. As soon as he was past the threshold, I used both hands to gather the salt back together to form a solid line again.

When I turned around, the four of them wore matching furrowed brows. Alice's eyes searched my face before she asked, "We're not alone, are we?"

With a shake of my head, I said, "No. We are in the presence of Jason Freelander."

Piper squinted as she searched around the room for Jason. "So, he was feeding you the information about your agent?"

"Yeah. Most of the time, spirits talk to me and tell me what's going on. There are always a few that are harder to read or want me to prove I'm worthy of getting their information. Those spirits make me work for the information. Jason, however, was a perfect informer and told me exactly what I needed to get rid of Jack," I confessed and smiled at Jason.

"So why can't we see him?" Hazel asked.

"Unfortunately, you don't have psychic abilities. Most people don't, or at least not enough to consistently see or experience ghost activities. I'd like to imagine most people have a little bit, but depending on what's going on in their life, it waxes and wanes like the moon. New ghosts are hard to see. Most of the time, they're invisible, even to me and other psychics. Older spirits will allow themselves to be seen. Bradley is a new spirit. He died almost a year ago," I answered.

"Since Jason couldn't get into the room, does that mean other spirits can't get in either?" Bear asked.

"That's correct," I said with a nod.

Bear's arm wrapped around Alice and pulled her in closer. I had realized that Bear wasn't one for long conversations days ago but recognized his daily actions and subtle affections displayed his fondness for her. He had been concerned that Alice would be spirited away in the night. Having confirmation that the salt lines were working made me take a sigh of relief as well. Of course I wanted my friends to be safe, but I didn't want to repeat my midnight trips to the cemetery either.

Piper and Hazel whispered to each other in the corner of the room. They were plotting something, but I didn't have time to try to figure out what they were up to. They each grabbed Alice and Bear's arms and dragged them to the adjoining room.

"What are you doing?" Alice yelled as she nearly tripped over her feet.

"We have agreed," Piper began.

"That you and Bear could use some time," Hazel continued.

"To talk and chat," Piper finished.

"We're going to stay with Cassandra tonight," Hazel added and smiled at me over her shoulder.

"But don't worry! We're going to salt up the room as a precaution," Piper said.

The four of them disappeared into the other room and I heard the sound of salt being shaken in containers like a maraca. When I peeked my head through the door, I could see they had made salt lines around the room.

"I'm all out," Hazel declared as she held up her canister of salt.

With wide eyes and jaw dropped, Bear said, "The three of you are going to share one bed."

"Yep! Don't you worry," Hazel replied brightly.

"This way there's no pressure on you two sharing a bed," Piper said. Then in a whisper, she added, "Not saying you can't share a bed. But the pressure isn't there."

Alice's face reddened to a deep shade of crimson. I walked to her and gave her a hug. "You do need to talk," I whispered.

She nodded slowly.

Piper and Hazel, once their preparations were completed, dragged me out of the room and said in unison, "Good night!"

They shut the door behind them. We heard the click of the lock on their side. I didn't blame them, especially with Hazel and Piper.

When their mischievous smiles crossed their faces again, I knew they weren't done for the night.

They ran to the front door and snuck out into the night. I followed to make sure they didn't get into too much trouble, but in reality I wanted to see what they were up to.

I found them peering through the window at Bear and Alice. As I peeked in, I saw that they had positioned the curtain inside so it opened a crack. They giggled as they spied.

I didn't want to be left out, so I stretched to my tip toes to see over their heads.

Alice and Bear were wrapped up in each other's embrace. Her arms were lifted with her fingers tangled in his hair. Their heads were bent toward each other and their lips locked in a kiss.

Then their hands were running up and down each other's bodies. I grabbed both Hazel and Piper by the arms and pulled them back from the window.

"We need to give them some privacy," I whispered.

"I'm glad it's cool out here," Hazel said. "It was getting hot."

Piper fanned herself. "I'm not sleeping in that room after this."

Back inside, we got ready for the night. It felt like a slumber party and we were all safe. Hazel and Piper laughed easily and smiled warmly. Piper played music I had never heard of before, while Hazel taught me how to do her twelve-step nighttime skin care routine. In my heart, I knew I would never have the patience to follow through with it myself, but it was fun to be pampered a little.

From a nearby motel room, someone knocked. Hazel and Piper didn't seem to notice so I ignored it, craving the girl time that I hadn't had much of in my life.

After the face masks and every inch of our bodies were covered in lotion, we fell into bed. Somehow, we all squeezed onto the queen-sized bed together, with Piper and Hazel on either side of me. It was a proper slumber party.

The last time I had shared a bed with someone where I had felt that crowded was with Zack. He had always crowded me and drooled on my pillows.

However, with these women, I felt like they held me in place. I was protected and safe.

I had never been so relaxed or calm.

Sleep found me within minutes and my worries slipped away. Almost instantly, I fell into my dreams.

They felt light and airy, nonsense, really. In my hazy thoughts, I realized it was a junk dream, and I settled in for whatever random and weird things my brain was trying to work through. My dream self was walking around shopping.

Bags filled my hands and they were getting heavy. It was a struggle to keep walking. My hands and arms were aching and threatening to drop the bags. I resisted dropping them, because whatever was inside was fragile.

Someone from behind me took a few out of my hands. When I turned to see who it was, I saw Alice. Then a group of people came and took more from my hands. Slowly, I recognized Hazel, Bear, and Piper. They each held some bags for me.

We continued walking together and made our way to a store that sold nothing but salt. Alice and I loaded the counter with containers of salt. Himalayan pink salt, black salt, and table salt overflowed.

Alice laughed, "Nothing will get past these!"

The world darkened around us and the lights overhead shut off and were plunged into darkness. Something wasn't right. My heart was pounding and not only in the dream. Panic forced me to wake and followed me from the dream.

The moment I sat up in bed, Bear began pounding on the adjoining door, yelling, "Alice is gone!"

Fourteen

All Hell Breaks Loose

Instantly, the three of us were up, and raced to open the door. Bear stood in front of us, shirtless, his hair and eyes wild.

"Where did she go?" I asked as I grabbed my shoes from the corner. Hazel and Piper left to go back to their room to get jackets and shoes as well.

"I have no idea. We were sleeping, and when I woke up she was gone. She's not outside. I even ran down the road to see if I could find her. Her side of the bed was cold," he said. In his hand, he tried to tap on the screen of his phone, but it didn't respond. "It was fully charged before we went to bed."

Hazel, Piper, and I checked our own phones and found them to be functioning.

"Spirits shouldn't have been able to get into the room," I said and pushed past Bear into the adjoining room.

"What do spirits have to do with phone batteries," Hazel

asked from the doorway.

Quickly, I replied, "Spirits will drain batteries if they're trying to show themselves to others or make their presence known."

On a mission, I inspected every inch of the salt line and searched for any imperfections.

When I got close to the entrance, my heart sank as I saw the break in the line. "A spirit got in," I said as I pointed to the salt.

Bear was ready to bound out the door to search for Alice, but I had a few questions for him first.

"Someone came here, didn't they?" I asked.

He nodded, "Zander. He was surprised to see Alice and I alone together. He thought she would be with you."

"What did he want?"

Bear shrugged. "He was uncomfortable and stumbled over his words. He told me that he wanted to apologize for how he acted, but he shifted a lot and rolled his eyes when he said the word "apologize."

Hazel piped up, "Zander has never apologized for anything a day in his life."

Bear nodded, "I agree. Even his mom can't make him apologize for his bad behavior. I don't understand why he started now."

I walked to the front door and knelt to inspect the salt. My heart sank as I looked at the break in the line. "I know why. To break the line so someone from this room could be taken."

Bear swore under his breath and said, "He paced around the room for a few minutes, apologized, and left. I didn't even notice that he had done anything to the line."

"Get what you need," I told the group. "I believe I know where Alice was taken. She's either bait in a trap to ensure I finally go to the cemetery or else she'll stand in for whatever they need me for."

"How can I help?" Jason asked.

"You can't come. It's too dangerous," I told him.

"Perhaps it's too dangerous to go without me," he replied.

Piper shifted her gaze between me and the empty space that Jason's voice echoed from. With a heavy sigh, she reached down and broke the salt line and said, "We don't have time for this. He can make his own decisions about whether to come or not."

Sirens wailed in the distance. It sounded as if every emergency vehicle was on their way somewhere. Something or someone was keeping them busy and I doubted that we would get help from the police until it was too late.

"I'm coming," Jason replied. There was no point in arguing with him.

Before we could leave, Bear ran to his car and pulled out a bunch of phone charging banks. He handed each of us one. "Some would say that I over prepare, but in moments like this, it's worth it."

Each of us connected our phones and stuffed them in pockets and purses. Hopefully, Bear's would charge enough before he needed his. For the rest of us, it would ensure they would stay charged if any spirits tried to drain them.

The three of us ran at full speed. Pain shot through my chest and my hands instantly came up to hold my boobs down. In our rush to leave, I hadn't thought of throwing on a bra.

As soon as my feet hit the road, there was a pull that told me to turn left to the cemetery. For the first time, I was going there without its guidance. I was going to find out what was in there.

Soon, we stood outside the cemetery.

Bear turned to us and asked, "Do you hear that?"

Hazel and Piper shook their heads. I nodded. "It's a high-pitched tone, but it sounds incredibly far away." The sirens were still sounding, but the tone was barely audible over them.

"That's what I've been hearing since Jack got here. We need to be careful," Jason said. "I'm going to see if I can sneak in with you, undetected." His translucent form faded and he disappeared from view.

Bear was the first of us to step onto the grounds. The light from the moon overhead cast shadows from the trees and gravestones. It felt like we were walking into a horror movie. I hoped we would all survive the night. The spirits inside the overfull cemetery stood every foot or two from each other. When I stepped onto the property, they instantly began to pull back.

"We need to stick together. No splitting up. Link arms if you have to. Don't fall over any of the stones or down any hills," Bear said as he led us. His arm linked with mine while Piper and Hazel walked behind us with their arms linked.

Bear scanned the area as he walked, almost as if he were tracking Alice's route. He led us through the twists and turns of the roads. As soon as we wandered away from the center of the cemetery, it became noticeably steep. On the hills were scattered gravestones. At the bottom of the hills, rows of stones were lined up neatly.

As we walked, I shivered and noticed that Bear had put on a shirt before we had left. The crisp autumn air had dropped drastically since the sun had set. Winter threatened to make an appearance early.

No one called out for Alice. We all knew that quiet would

be best. The fallen leaves crunched and rustled under our feet as we walked, which defeated our efforts.

The cemetery was larger than it appeared from the road. Between the cluster of trees and the steep hills at the back, the cemetery's true size was hidden from view.

Bear walked straight to the back, ignoring the area to the left of us. Perhaps he was guided by the same force that had focused its energy on me over the past week or so. Perhaps it was pure love for Alice that influenced him. I suspected it was love.

We followed the road as it wound around the top of the hill and veered to the left. A line of trees surrounded the cemetery and there was nowhere else to go ahead of us. Bear powered on.

Whatever guided him, led him straight to her.

From our vantage point on top of the hill, we could see a giant pentagram carved into the earth below us. The ruts were deep and led to each point in the star. On one of the points, Alice stood fixed in place. She didn't acknowledge us. Bear ran down the hill to her before I could stop him.

Quickly, I glanced up at the stars to see which direction the top of the pentagram was pointing.

"Be careful. It's pointing south. Something wicked is here," I said softly. The rest of us made our way down the hill slowly. Despite our caution, Hazel slipped and slid a few feet.

When we were finally at the base, I whispered, "Let's get Alice out of here."

From on top of the hill, Jason cried out. "Watch out!" I could hear him grunting and struggling. "Let go!" he hissed.

"Jason!" I called, but he didn't reply. "I'd like to find the asshole who keeps taking my ghosts."

I heard a man's deep voice utter, "Now, that's not how to make first impressions, my dear."

Startled, I jerked around. For a brief moment, I thought it had been Bradley.

Instead, a tall milky white man walked out from behind the tree line. Had he taken Alice, knowing we would come for her? The moment he reached a patch of moonlight, his pale bare chest was accentuated by the dim light. He wore a long flowing black jacket over a pair of black flowy pants. A shock of white hair almost glowed in the night. In his right hand, he held a wooden flute.

Whatever veil he used to hide his presence from me fell. Waves of nausea overcame me, and I fell to my knees. Pure evil pulsed from him.

He was nothing I had ever dealt with before.

"Who are you?" I struggled to ask. Behind the man, Bear called to Alice, but she did not respond. He even attempted to pick her up, but her feet were firmly grounded to the spot.

"Your worst nightmare," he replied. I didn't get any powerful auras from him. As far as I could tell, he was simply a human. However, the flute radiated with energy.

Something rustled in the tree line and leaves crunched under someone's feet. The light from a flashlight cut through the darkness. Slowly, with heaving breaths, Zander emerged on the edge of the pentagram.

He ran over and out of breath said, "Hey, Doyle! I got everything set up. Digging the star was hard. The police will be occupied all night. Thanks to a night of shooting this thing off." He held up a gun and tried to spin it on his finger, but it flung off and hit the ground. Luckily, it didn't go off.

The glare that Doyle shot could have incinerated Zander.

"So, Doyle, was it?" I asked. "Why don't you tell us what you want? And Zander, how long have you been doing this weirdos' dirty work?"

He sneered at me and ambled toward me. "I give orders and don't answer questions. You're going to do exactly what I say, otherwise I'll work my magic on her, like I did with Zander. Besides, I've got your ghost. You've started a collection yourself. Perhaps we're more alike than either of us realize." Doyle swept his hand in a large circle and emphasized how many ghosts he too had gathered. When he was face to face with me he whispered, "What's up with you and the ghosts in your motel room? Do you get frisky with them? Is that a thing?"

With a sigh of frustration I said, "It's not a thing. They're my friends. Where are they? I couldn't see Bradley before so how can I tell you haven't harmed him? And now Jason seems to have been taken now too!"

Doyle didn't answer but laughed at me instead.

Zander moved closer to Piper and Hazel, shone the flashlight into their faces and snarled, "Bet you wish you had been kinder to me, huh?"

"How long have you been working with Boyle?" I asked.

"It's Doyle," Doyle and Zander said in unison.

With a mischievous smile, I replied, "My mistake. How long have you been with him?"

Zander sneered, "It was after I left the sleep over. He called to me." Then his tone softened. "Or played to me. The flute was impossible to resist."

Doyle turned away from me for a moment, but his rage emanated off of him. With a quick spin, he turned and slapped me across the face. The force of the hit sent me to the ground.

My cheek burned, like he had fire in his hands. "You're far too nosy," Doyle said.

Piper and Hazel rushed over to me and helped me back to my feet.

"What do you want with us?" Hazel asked softly.

A wicked smile broke through Doyle's anger and he announced, "I'm going to use you all to summon the woman of my dreams. She's haunted me for years. Tonight, finally, all the pieces have aligned."

From behind us, I heard Bradley's voice, "Cassandra, whatever you do, do *not* help him." Then his cry rang out through the cemetery and he was silent again.

With a quiver in my voice, I asked, "Who is this dream woman of yours?"

"Dolores," Doyle said with a hint of a sigh. "Take them, Zander. The time is growing late."

Piper, Hazel, and I glanced at each other for a brief second, then at the same time, we bolted. Behind us, Zander chased and gained ground on us. Hazel was slower and he reached her first, tackling her to the ground. In an instant, Piper and I stopped to help her.

We pulled on his arms, digging our fingernails into him. He screamed and Hazel kicked him in the balls. She scrambled from under him and we raced away. The entry to the cemetery was yards away from us so we picked up speed.

Cold, icy hands wrapped around my biceps and halted me in an instant. The spirits that resided in the cemetery surrounded us. Hazel and Piper were dragged away from me, back toward the hill. Their yells and screams echoed in the night. I pulled and yanked against the hands, but their grip stayed fast on my arms.

I was able to catch one last glimpse of Piper as she was thrown down the hill with Hazel close behind her.

As soon as they were out of view, my world went dark and I felt myself hit the ground.

Fifteen

Dangerous Type

When the world came back to me, I was standing in the center of the pentagram, supported by the invisible hands of the spirits that captured us. Hazel, Piper, and Alice were placed on the points of the star where they too were held up by invisible hands. They were all unconscious. Bear was nowhere in sight. Maybe he could find someone to help, but my mind was blank as to who would be able to offer any assistance in this situation.

There were two points on the star that were empty. If one was set aside for Bear, I wondered, "Who was going to take the second? Certainly not Doyle."

I could almost hear my mom's voice remind me that as long as the points of the star were not filled, he wouldn't be able to proceed forward with the summoning. Throughout my childhood and adolescence, she had complimented our public education with less conventional topics like witchcraft, tarot card reading, meditation, and cryptozoology.

Doyle snarled at Zander, "Go find your friend, now!"

Like a dog that had scented a fox, he took off into the night. What seemed like hours ticked by without Zander returning.

Doyle slowly circled the star but remained silent.

Around the circle, spirits stood shoulder to shoulder. They had a variety of visibility to me. The youngest being diaphanous while the older spirits were apparitions, their bodies almost solid.

Hazel began to slowly move as she woke. She struggled against the invisible hands holding her in place. With wide eyes, she finally focused on me.

"Are we going to die?" she cried as tears fell down her face.

Internally, I struggled. Did I tell her there was hope that we would get out of the cemetery unscathed? Or did I tell her the truth, that if Bear was captured, we were going to die. "I don't know," I said softly and met Doyle's eyes to get any insight from him. He didn't seem to be inclined to share his plans with me. With a neutral face, he continued to circle us.

Piper's chin was still to her chest and showed no sign of waking. Alice stood still, eyes wide but unseeing. She was under the effect of whatever Doyle had done to her.

From Doyle's pocket his phone rang, loud and clear. Quickly, he retrieved it and dashed away toward the road above us. My best guess was that he was leading someone to us or he needed better reception. Either way, it gave me time to work against the spirits.

I tried to move my wrists and tug against the hands, but the spirits grip on me was true. "Talk to me, please," I whispered to the spirits. "What has he done to you?"

They were silent.

Again, I tried. "If you can't let me go, let Bradley and Jason go. They're like you. Innocent of this."

A spirit near Alice shifted and I knew I had found the weak link in their chain. With my eyes closed, I concentrated harder than I ever had before. I searched for feelings, names, and details that may be whispered.

In my mind's eye, I could sense a ribbon of energy that emitted from me. With great focus, I found I could reach the ribbon out to the shifty spirit. Gently, I tapped him on the shoulder and caressed them slowly. Icy touches were normal when coming in contact with a spirit, but the moment my energy touched the spirit, a blast of arctic air ran straight through the ribbon and into my physical body.

I pushed through the ice and refused to retreat from him. Through the ribbon, I sent warm, kind thoughts. "You didn't deserve to be disturbed like this. You deserve rest and quiet." Over and over, I sent the chant to him. Slowly, I could see the glow of a white sphere, a warm and bright light building around him.

Almost like when a sheet of ice gets warmed by the sun, I sensed cracks in the arctic cold around the spirit. I increased the warmth and began sending a question. "Who are you?"

When Doyle's hold on the spirit broke, a blast of freezing air shot out in a circle, hitting us all. Alice blinked slowly as if she were finally coming back to herself. She shivered as she took in her surroundings. Piper opened her eyes and instantly her chest began to heave while her mouth was pressed into a fine line.

Alice began to cry and leaned on the hands that were holding her up, as if her legs were weak. Piper's knees wobbled a little, but she kept herself upright and pulled against the hands.

Hazel whispered a "Shhh," to the group and she nodded at me.

Again, I sent warmth and light to the spirit. "Who are you? Please tell me," I asked through the ribbon.

For long moments, I waited for his response. Right as I began to lose hope that he would answer, the name, "William," rang true. It was not soft and quiet. It was loud and everyone in the group heard his name. Their heads turned toward the sound. William's spiritual body seemed to come into focus more, letting everyone see him.

"William. Thank you for telling us your name," I said through the ribbon. "What holds you here?"

"Doyle. He raised me from my sleep. I've been dead over fifty years. He is not a person I would ever associate with," William replied with a sniff. He stood taller than many of the other spirits I could see. "Most of us here would never have chosen this association."

"I have sensed that," I said. "Help us and let us go. We won't let him raise Dolores."

William shook his head slowly. "He holds us here. Until he releases us, we are at his will."

"What about Bradley and Jason? Where are they?" I asked frantically.

"They are being held until they submit. If they resist too long, he's threatened to send us to take Dolores' place in her prison. There's no peace, only torture where she's being held," William replied softly.

Around the circle, other spirits began to shake their heads, as if they too were slowly regaining their voices. "Where is Dolores being held?"

William shook his head, "We don't speak of it. Just know

that no spirit would willingly go there."

I nodded, "Thank you. I will release all of you from this hold as quickly as possible. Whether you stay or go, will be your decision. I appreciate whatever help you can give us."

In the distance, Doyle's voice rang through the night. "Ah, finally, we are all set." He came into view moments later, his bright white smile almost glowing in the night.

From behind Doyle, Bear's form appeared, held in place with invisible hands. He struggled and fought against the spirits that held him. Their strength overpowered Bear and slowly, they positioned him over one of the empty points of the star.

Doyle beckoned Zander to the edge of the woods.

Thwack.

Moments later, Doyle returned with Zander being dragged by invisible hands. His head lolled to one side and a red lump began to form on his forehead. Gently, the spirits placed him on the final point.

We had failed and weren't prepared for Doyle. Whoever Dolores was, she was bad news. I needed time, to think, to stall, to stop her from manifesting. I had to focus on anything besides the growing hopelessness in my chest. No one was going to save us. Not any of the ghosts, including Bradley or Jason. If I let the despair take over, we would be dead within the hour.

I blurted, "Tell me more about Dolores."

Doyle smiled wickedly and sauntered closer to me, avoiding even a toe onto the circle. "Why tell you, when I can show you?" He cackled as he brought his hands above his head and began to chant.

Before I could comprehend what he was saying, my world grew fuzzy and my ears rang.

And just like the magic girl anime and 80's cartoons that I grew up watching, each of my friends, and Zander, emitted a glowing, pulsing color of light from their chests. Pink from Alice, yellow from Piper, green from Hazel, blue from Bear, and red from Zander. But there was no Captain Planet or Sailor Moon to help us now.

Slowly, their color began to seep out of each of them and formed a ribbon of energy. Their colors twisted and curled slowly in the air.

Instead of going to Doyle, as I had expected, the ribbons reached toward me. The moment Alice's pink ribbon touched my skin, a jolt zapped through my body and a warm glow emanated from my chest.

Then Bear's ribbon reached me, another jolt zapped through me and the glow grew brighter. With each touch of a ribbon, I was met with another jolt and an increase in the glow from my chest.

Something moving above us caught my eye and I stared up at a swirling black and blue whirlpool in the sky. The ringing in my ears blocked out every other sound. Alice's mouth was open in a wide, silent scream. Doyle's mouth moved as he continued to chant, his eyes closed.

From the space in front of me, a form took shape. She was hunched over. Her face was obscured behind her greasy hair that hung in snarled clumps. Her torn and dirty clothing clung to her gray tinted skin. With one wrinkled hand that was covered in liver spots, she pulled her hair back from her face.

Dolores' face was old and ragged. One of her dark brown eyes drooped heavily and showed deep red blood vessels in the whites.

Doyle opened his eyes, a smile on his face as he saw Dolores had appeared, but instantly, his delight turned to horror. I could read his lips as he repeated over and over, "What?" His hands found his hair, and he began pulling and tugging at it.

Her hoarse voice croaked out, "Keep up the spell, dearest."

With a quiver at his lips, he returned to his chants.

The ribbons of light from around the circle continued to flow into me.

As I glanced over to my shoulder, the invisible hand that held me in place slowly shifted into focus. First the outline, then solid. With a gasp, I saw the full form of a young woman. Her long wavy blonde hair fell perfectly over her shoulders and onto a flowing white dress with bell sleeves.

The pressure she held on my upper left arm released as she held up her hand in front of her face.

Around the circle, the spirits holding the others in place had become visible. Not only visible, but had become solid, exactly as Dolores was becoming by the minute.

As soon as Doyle saw the spirits, he smiled wickedly and began a new chant. Then the spirits within the circle fell to the ground. They scratched at their arms and scalps as they shrieked in pain. Their fingers pulled at their hair. Slowly, chunks of skin began to fall from their faces and hands. Flashes of white bone shone in the moonlight overhead.

I saw my chance. Tentatively, I took a step off the spot where I had been rooted and found my movement was no longer impeded. Tearing hell for leather, I ran to Alice and tried to free her from her spot. She didn't respond to my call to her, so I rubbed my hands up and down her arms.

As soon as my icy fingers touched her skin, she shivered. Her eyes focused on me, and she nodded her head toward her pocket.

"What?" I shouted over the sound. "What's in there?"

Her hand tapped on her pocket. When I slipped my hand in and I grasped a glass vial. I glanced back up at Alice in time to see her mouth the words, "Watch out!"

Sixteen

Only the Lonely

Dolores' wrinkly, liver spotted hand grasped my shoulder. Her long sharp nails dug in until I was sure she had drawn blood. I cried out and popped open the vial still clutched in my hand. With all the force I could muster, I swung my arm up and hit Dolores in the face. Holy water dripped down her cheeks and in surprise, she let go of my shoulder.

"Why does that sting?" she croaked in my ear.

Without answering, I dashed away from her but was unable to push past the spirits surrounding the circle. Even if I could have gotten away, the ribbons that followed me would have revealed my location. I needed to interrupt the spell somehow.

Quickly, I glanced around the circle. Alice and Bear, finally released from the spirit hold, ran to each other. As soon as they were close enough, their hands clasped together. Piper wobbled on her feet, no longer bound but lacking strength to move. Hazel had slumped to the ground, unconscious again. Zander sat on the ground while he rubbed his forehead.

Bear picked up Hazel from the ground while Alice and I approached Piper. With both of her arms around our necks, we supported Piper and moved her off of her spot. But we were trapped.

As we moved closer to the edge of the circle, Alice pounded on the barrier around us. None of the spirits moved or released us. Bear, in frustration, kicked the barrier with his foot.

Dolores wiped at her eyes and began to walk toward me again. With a quick glance, I noticed Doyle's legs had begun to shake. In an instant, one of his knees gave out. He released a loud groan as he hit the ground.

Between the spell and the hold that he had on the spirits his energy was tapped. Instantly, the spirits released their ranks around us. The wall evaporated. The ribbons of energy from my friends cracked and broke into pieces, scattering the earth with shard remnants. Slowly, the shards began to dissolve, leaving behind a rainbow of droplets on the ground.

The spirits dashed away and escaped as far away as they could to avoid being used by Doyle again.

In my ear, someone grumbled and I knew instantly who it was.

"Bradley!" I whispered.

"Took you long enough to come find me," he complained.

"I didn't know where you were," I said.

"That's kinda the point when you're kidnapped," he replied.

"Ghostnapped," I added.

Bradley said, "Get out of here."

Ahead of us was a steep hill with no cover. That side of the cemetery was free of gravestones. Behind us was the woods.

We chose the woods and left Zander behind.

Dolores hobbled to stand over Doyle and he recoiled. Her voice carried on the wind even though it sounded like a whisper. "Dearest. Don't you like my visage? Isn't it all you ever dreamed about? For months, you've told me how ravishing I was. Where are those words of endearment now?"

He shook his head and he scooted himself back from her. Dolores matched his every retreating inch with a step forward. "This isn't what you were supposed to look like. You were young and beautiful. Not a hollowed out old corpse," he said.

"My love. You promised me a *complete* ceremony. That would have given me all the beauty that I promised you, but you failed on your side. You let me down," she replied, her harsh words as coarse as her voice. With her hand held over Doyle, Dolores released a sound somewhere between a scream and a gasp for breath.

Doyle's body arched against the cold, hard ground. His fingers bent and scratched like he was clawing at something above him we could not see. His inhuman screams echoed into the night and were met with howls of wolves and barking of dogs.

When his breath rattled in his chest, Dolores knelt and pressed her lips to his. Instead of the kiss I was expecting, she suctioned her mouth over his and inhaled.

His body grew limp as she consumed his escaping energy.

My eyes were transfixed on the nightmare ahead of me. I should have run, but my knees wobbled at the mere thought of movement, like a rabbit trying to hide from a predator. When she was done, Doyle's body was only a pile of dust. The breeze blew for a moment and picked up bits of the debris and scattered him.

In an instant, I felt myself being dragged backward, away from Dolores. A hand clamped over my mouth, muffling my surprised cry. In my ear, Bear's soft voice said, "It's us. We gotta get out of here."

While I had been preoccupied with Dolores, Hazel and Piper had recovered and both were standing on their own. We needed to get to a road. The woods would hide us until we did.

Slower than what I would have liked, we traveled deeper into the trees. Bear led us through, but the crunch of leaves under our feet would alert Dolores of where we were.

"Either we need to find one place to hide or need to get out of here. We're making too much noise with all these leaves," Bear whispered to us.

We all nodded at him, and he began to move us around the edge of the cemetery, until we would be closer to the road.

In the moonlight, an old park bench sat, its seat covered in tree sap and stained green from years of fallen leaves. Bear positioned us behind it and pointed up.

"We have to climb up a hill inside the tree line. Get ready to run," he said softly.

On the wind, Dolores' voice whispered, "I am free. Cassandra, you cannot get away from me."

We rushed forward. Fear and panic drove us to move quicker than what our bodies were capable of. The hill was steeper than I had anticipated, and almost instantly my calves burned. Piper stumbled and Alice tumbled to the ground. Bear, in an instant, was by her side and helped her upright again. I tripped on a rock but caught myself on a tree nearby.

Piper aimed for the trees and used them to lean her body on as she ascended. Hazel used her hands and knees to crawl up the side of the hill. Slowly, we each made it to the top, within the tree line.

Dolores was nowhere in sight.

While we could not see the road, every once in a while the sound of a passing vehicle let us know we were close. Quietly, we each took a step out of the trees and into the moonlight.

Bear pointed at the gravestones and whispered, "Hide behind them as we go."

One by one we dashed to a headstone and crouched in their shadows in an effort to hide ourselves. It almost felt like the air was fresher the further we got from Dolores. My energy felt like it was being replenished with each deep breath.

From grave to grave, we hid in the shadows until we finally could see the road.

Bear reached for Alice and together they raced out of the cemetery. On the side of the road, they beckoned us to join them. Piper was the next to make the dash followed closely by Hazel. When they were almost to the fence, I felt hands on my shoulders. They pulled me back and down hard. My body and head hit the ground and my vision grew fuzzy.

Seventeen

Pit of Despair

"Zander! You can never come back from this!" someone shouted. I didn't care to find out what was going on. My head hurt and the act of opening my eyes was difficult. Sleep seemed more inviting. Maybe I would perk up in the morning and could sort out what was going on then.

"I don't care! Doyle understood me that night. He found me and felt my pain. None of you even came to find me. None of you cared when I didn't respond to texts. I was forgotten the moment I walked out that motel room door," Zander yelled. "But Doyle and Dolores promised me everything I could ever want. Power. Knowledge. Control. All you've ever done was mock me."

Was that Zander? Why was he so loud and angry? Weren't we all friends?

"You have been our friend for years. But what you've done is irreparable," a woman shouted. Was there a train nearby? It was so loud. The sound and shouting were making it difficult for me to sleep.

"No. I believe you've got that wrong. You were short-sighted and now don't like the consequences," the man shouted again. I searched for sleep, searched for my dreams and quiet, but they evaded me. It was like when I wake up at midnight but am unable to fall back to sleep despite being tired.

But I wasn't in my bed. There were rocks and gravel under me. My fingers traced the ground. Where was I laying that was so hard and rough? Had I been sleepwalking somewhere? When I turned my head slightly, pain boomed and pounded without mercy.

And I remembered. Memories of the past few hours came flooding back, each replaying in my mind. There was no sleep or rest for me now. I opened my eyes to see Hazel held by Zander with a knife against her throat. His blade was dangerously close to cutting her flesh.

Inch by inch, I rose from my prone position to sit. Despite the pain, I moved slowly and steadily.

"Be careful," Bradley's voice whispered in my ear. "Dolores is waiting for everyone back at the pentagram."

We were alone. No one was going to save us from Zander and Dolores.

Bear held up a hand toward Zander. "Zander, we've been buds since I moved here. There's still time to stop this before it's too late."

Slowly, Zander took a step back from Bear. "What penance have you done? What apologies have you made to me?"

Bear took another step toward Zander. "Just let Hazel go. You can take me."

A loud boom of laughter broke from Zander. "You're taller

and stronger than I am Bear. We've wrestled enough for me to know that I can never win against you. But Hazel here," he said and nodded his head at her. "She's much easier to move. And she makes a better hostage to make all of you comply."

Piper whispered, "Don't hurt her."

Slowly, Zander took a step back. Then another. "That I can't promise. Rest assured that I'm not going to kill her. However, Hazel doesn't need to be conscious to finish the ritual," he snarled with hatred dripping from his voice.

He lifted the knife from her throat and made a motion to hit her over the head with the hilt, but she stomped on his foot with all her might. When his grip loosened on her, she turned and kneed him in the groin.

Hazel ran away from him and into Piper's arms. Quickly, they joined Bear and Alice on the road behind me. I slowly got off the ground, but my feet and legs felt heavy. There was no speed I could summon.

Zander was up and had his hands wrapped around my arms before I was near my friends. I twisted and turned to break free. He laughed at my attempts and his awful smile lit up his face. "You're caught. There's no way out for you. Dolores needs you. You'll be rewarded for your service," he parroted.

I shook my head and said, "I don't know who Dolores is. Or what she is. I suspect she's never been human."

He cackled before he replied, "Nothing gets past you, huh? Dolores is a goddess. As soon as you complete the ritual, she will be restored to her former glory."

"Essentially, she needed more than me. She needed all six of us. And I do believe that they've left the cemetery," I replied. I locked eyes with the group that stood on the road and yelled to them, "You will *not* step another foot into this cemetery until she has been returned to wherever she came."

They each nodded at me and I hoped they understood that they could not return for me, no matter what happened.

Without another word, Zander grabbed my wrist and wrestled me back to Dolores.

I heard Alice yell, "No! Bear you can't go!"

No matter what, they could not come for me. I only hoped that they would listen.

When Zander pulled me next to the hill, his hands released me and pushed me. Head over heels, I rolled down. By the time I reached the bottom, I was dizzy.

Dolores began to walk toward me and began to clap. "I knew I could count on you, Zander."

He ran down the hill .

"You don't have everyone you need," I announced with more confidence than I felt.

Zander held me tightly and in place in the exact center of the star. The cemetery no longer felt overrun by spirits. Now, there were only two spirits I could sense, and I knew exactly who they were.

Bradley and Jason hadn't left me.

Dolores carefully stepped over the ruts in the ground until she stood above me. I noticed that her hair was fuller than it had been when she first appeared. And it could have been the darkness, but she no longer appeared to be as old as before. Instead of resembling a thousand-year- old mummy, now, she appeared closer to only being about a hundred.

Her cold, bony hands gripped my chin. "Oh, I'll get them soon enough. I don't need you all together. I've got their scents now. Once I'm done with you, I'll leave this cemetery and suck them dry of their energy." Her jagged fingernails dug into my flesh and forcibly turned my head side to side. With a hiss she added, "This is the best you could bring me, Zandy? I would have preferred a younger body. This one is middle aged."

A disgusted gasp escaped me. I had never been so insulted in my life. For someone to actually call me middle aged was outrageous. I wasn't even forty yet! "At least I look better than you!" I snared.

She clicked her tongue and added, "Honey, see what you look like in a few centuries. Oh well. Beggars can't be choosers, right?"

Dolores let go of my chin and grasped both of my shoulders with her hands, fingernails digging into the joint. She let her head fall back and pointed her face to the sky above us.

Something pulled from my body and made me gasp. From my chest, a single silver string emerged. It floated straight to Dolores and began to wrap around her legs, like a spool of thread filling up a bobbin on a sewing machine.

I watched as the thread covered one of her legs, wrapped around her center, and moved down to her other leg. She was going to become a mummy wrapped in my essence.

In desperation, I yelled to Bradley and Jason. "Make sure my family knows where I'm at." The thought of my parents and sisters wondering what happened to me made me nauseous. Having my soul sucked from my body didn't help the sensation.

Neither of the spirits replied, but that was for the best.

After Dolores' second leg was covered, the thread moved to her torso.

Within minutes, her torso and arms were covered. The only thing left was her head.

Eighteen

As The World Falls Down

A strange bird call broke through the night. Zander, still holding me in place, began to laugh. "That's the weirdest sound I've ever heard. Sounds like someone is trying to kill that bird." Into the night, he yelled, "Kill it and get it over with." His entire body shook with his laughter.

He wasn't paying attention to me. Or at least not as closely now.

In my mind's eye, I replayed the moment Hazel stomped on his foot. Then I repeated what she had done. A hard slam to the same foot and a knee to the groin. Getting kneed three times in close succession would hopefully take him down longer.

Quickly, I leapt out of the circle like I was a runner in baseball, sliding into home base. An added benefit was some of the dirt and ground filled in the ruts as I slid over it. The circle was broken. It would be an easy fix, but something that would take time to do if they wanted to complete their ritual.

The moment I broke the circle, the thread broke off right as it began to wrap around her nose and cheeks. It would have only been a few more minutes before her head was fully covered.

An inhuman scream escaped her. "Of all the people these incompetent fools could have brought me, they brought you," she shouted.

I scrambled back from her and raced into a grove of trees. Desperate for a short rest, I hid behind one for a moment. In the distance, Dolores shone with my silver thread. She marveled at her arms as she lifted them in front of her face. Then slowly, the shine dissipated and soon was gone.

It was only a matter of time before Dolores found me. My time had run out, and I needed to get out of the cemetery. With all the force I could muster, I bolted up the hill. Almost instantly, my legs revolted and threatened to give out under me. The entrance to the cemetery was still so far away.

With the use of the trees, I crawled up the hill. The moment I reached the top, I collapsed to the ground. My chest heaved and it felt like I couldn't get enough air.

In the distance, I could hear Dolores. "Come out, come out, wherever you are."

I needed to get up. With more effort than I had ever expended before, I pushed myself to stand. Under my shoes, gravel crunched from the road. The sound gave me something else to focus on besides the ache and weakness all over my body.

Crunch. Crunch. Crunch. Deep breath. Crunch. Crunch. Crunch.

Quicker steps came from behind me.

A speedy glance over my shoulder showed Dolores running

inhumanly fast behind me. She was like a bulldozer with her sights set on me. My body refused to move any quicker.

I found myself on the ground, knees and palms dotted with new cuts and scrapes. With nowhere to hide, it felt like I had a spotlight on me as the moon shone light all around me. Dolores approached me, laughing. "You cannot run as far when you are an old husk of your former self."

As she stood over me, her foot swung out and kicked me in the ribs. My breath caught, and I crumpled to the ground. In the fetal position, I covered my head with my arms and peeked up at her.

Dolores no longer reminded me of King Tut's great grand-mother. The skin on her hands, arms, and neck was youthful. Her face, however, was truly frightening.

Where the thread had begun to wind, her skin appeared rejuvenated, highlighting how saggy and wrinkled the area above remained. Her eyes were bloodshot and hair hung limply. This close to her I could see bald spots on her head when her hair shifted.

From a tattered pocket, Dolores pulled a wooden flute.

"Don't worry. We'll reunite you with all of your spirit friends soon. You'll need an entourage to escort you down to hell. My keepers are going to start to wonder where I'm at," she said.

Slowly, she put the flute to her lips and gently blew over the mouthpiece. Light, airy sounds escaped from the end of the instrument. Her body swayed as she played and her eyes closed.

My thoughts shifted to Bradley and Jason, and I yelled, "Guys, get out of here." When I didn't hear any response, I hoped they took the warning and fled. Perhaps, they would get the other spirits far enough away that they wouldn't be enticed by her music.

A lump rose in my throat and I noticed I was extremely thirsty. My friends had obeyed my warnings and had not come to my rescue. I had saved them, but no one was going to save me now. It's what I had wanted but didn't make the realization that I was alone any easier.

Or that I was going to die alone.

For several minutes, Dolores played the flute, and I laid on the ground. My body refused to get up.

"What did you do to me?" I asked between my gasping breaths.

Delores played a few notes more, before she stopped to answer me. "I thought it was quite obvious. I have drained your youth and vitality, along with that of your friends. It takes a *lot* of energy to revive the dead. A cemetery full of spirits to guide my way here. Five living souls to fuel the host. And you. The host."

My hands shook as I touched my face to find wrinkles and folds that had never been there before. With my best glare I could conjure, I stared at Dolores.

That's when I noticed a small red birthmark on her left hand, close to her thumb. It was located exactly where I had one. When I glanced down at my hand, I shrieked.

My red birthmark was gone. In its place was wrinkled skin with liver spots.

Dolores laughed when she saw me searching my hand. "You're finally figuring this out, huh," she cackled. The flute was pressed back to her lips and she played again. She closed her eyes and swayed to her music.

With stiff legs and joints, I pushed myself to stand, but my legs didn't respond how they used to. Instead, I settled for sitting up. Slowly, I began to scoot across the gravel. The rocks dug into my hands and legs, but I endured the pain. A gravestone was only a few yards ahead. I could make it. Dolores didn't seem to notice or care about my movements.

As soon as I was close enough, I wrapped my hands around the stone. With its support, I hauled myself to my feet. My legs wobbled, as I slowly rose from the ground. As long as I held onto the granite, I remained upright. My vision swam and my heart pounded as if I had run a marathon.

I felt old. Older than Mrs. Koch.

Dolores' music continued to weave its way through the cemetery. None of the spirits showed themselves. She lowered the flute and shook her head. "Since no one wants to play right now, I guess I'll need to finish playing with my food. The magic of the moon is almost done," she said.

She began to walk toward me. I tried to add more space between us by taking a step backward, but the gravestones were obstacles that were difficult for me to navigate.

Clack.

Clack.

Clack.

Something hit the ground around Dolores. Rocks, I finally realized. Someone was throwing rocks. When I searched the darkness for the culprit, I couldn't find anyone.

Then a barrage of rocks and gravel hit the ground, like rapid fire.

"Ow!" Dolores screeched and grasped her face. She had finally been hit by one of the assaulting rocks.

I felt rooted in place as my joints ached and refused to budge from their spot.

Dolores screamed as the rocks continued to pummel her.

In my ear, I heard Jason whisper, "Cassandra, you need to move."

"I can't. I feel so old," I said wearily. If I sat down at that moment, I felt like I would fall asleep instantly.

Bradley grumbled next to me but didn't add anything.

Dolores refocused her attention onto me and approached. My stolen energy radiated off of her. Her arms spread wide and she cackled. Rocks continued to hit her, but she began to chant.

A string of words I didn't understand spewed from her mouth, and I felt the tug again. A silvery string sprang from my chest, winding its way from me. It stretched toward Dolores.

Before the string could go further, it stopped within my arms reach. It hovered in space and waved softly in the breeze back and forth.

Dolores screamed and repeated the strange words again, with more venom in her tone.

The string did not lengthen.

When she realized she could not persuade the string to go further, she released her arms to her side and stormed to me.

Fingers stretched out to grasp the string, but something blocked her. She scratched at whatever was before her but made no progress. Repeatedly, she tried to get the string, but it remained unreachable.

Bradley's voice said, "We've got you, Cassandra."

Jason added, "She has to go through us to get to you."

Tears sprang to my eyes as I realized what my two ghost companions had done. Together, they had formed an energy barrier and successfully blocked Dolores. I hadn't known spirits could do that.

That's when someone from the shadows tackled Dolores

and sent her to the ground.

Nineteen

Relax. It's Only Magic

I could see Bear struggling to hold Dolores down, through the growing light behind the trees. His hands pressed down on her arms to prevent her from moving. "Run!" he shouted.

Dolores screamed at Bear as she struggled to break free from his grasp. Quickly, he lifted one hand from her, made a tight fist, and brought it down onto her face. Instantly, she stopped moving.

Despite my shaky legs, I tried to take a step back but knew I was going to fall the moment a gravestone wasn't within reach.

Jason and Bradley whispered to each other, their invisible forms right in front of me.

"She needs to run," Jason said.

Bradley's signature grumble came before his response, "Yes. I agree, but she can't go around looking like that. We've got to get her life source back from Dolores. And sunrise will be here soon. With my limited knowledge of the paranormal, I'd guess we need to hurry to get this fixed."

"Last time I checked none of us are sorcerers or magic wielders. What weird language was she even speaking before? Alive is better than dead, regardless of how she looks," Jason countered.

"I'm standing right here," I hissed.

Bear whispered, "Dolores is alive, but unconscious."

The thread still hung in the air and searched for its place to go. Tentatively, I grasped another gravestone and took a step closer to Dolores. The ghost barrier was still in place.

I reached a hand out and closed my eyes. With my mind, I searched for Dolores. Her red-hot anger felt like it was bubbling under the surface. She was still *alive,* if that's how you could describe her existence.

Another slow step brought me closer to the moss-covered bench. Thankful for its presence, I sat down and was able to rest my legs. Without the pressure of standing, I envisioned one of my hands reaching her.

I could almost hear her screaming. "Her body may be unconscious, but her mind is very much active. She knows that I'm exploring her," I told my friends.

As my psychic hand touched her foot, I recognized an energy that could only have been mine. It was familiar and warm. Like home.

With my mind, I tried to pick a piece of the energy off of Dolores. A tiny silver string released from her and drifted slightly in the breeze. It glinted as I gently tugged but refused to unravel further. No matter how hard I pulled, it could not be free of Dolores.

"Where's Piper, Hazel, and Alice," I asked Bear.

From behind a mausoleum, the trio stepped out.

"Of course, you didn't listen to me," I said as I waved them over. "I have an idea. We need to move Dolores to the pentagram.

"Are you serious?," Bear asked. "We need to get out of here!"

"Yeah. What is she going to do when she's awake again? Do you believe she won't wreak havoc on us? The town? The spirits? She says she has all of your scents and will hunt you down. It's not safe for anyone while she's here. We need to send her back," I said.

"But we don't know how to do it," Hazel replied.

"True, but if we dial a friend, we may get some assistance," I said.

Bear picked up Dolores and disappeared ahead of us. Slowly, I followed, with my arms hung over both Alice and Piper's shoulders. They slowly helped me back to the pentagram. By the time we reached it, Bear had placed Dolores in the center near Zander's limp form splayed on the ground.

Sheepishly, Bear confessed, "I took care of Zander so he couldn't come assist Dolores. He's alive, don't worry. He's going to wake up with a pretty gnarly headache, though."

I nodded and asked, "What are everyone's phone percentages at? Have they been charging?"

Each of my friends checked their phones. Alice said, "I grabbed Zander's." All of our phones were over 50%.

"Let's hope that will be enough," I said. "You all need to call me."

One after another, they called my phone and I merged their calls into one. Then, I called my mother.

"Mom, please hold."

Then I called my dad. "Hey Dad. Hold on a second."

Then Ilona and Diana. "Don't hang up on me."

As soon as everyone was connected I announced, "Hey everyone! We've got nine people on this call. Mom, I promise I will give you a full run-down of everything that's happened to get me into trouble, but that will have to wait until I get home. Right now, we're dealing with a spirit who has returned to a body, using my energy. What we need help with is one: retrieving my life source from her and two: send her back to wherever she came from."

Ilona answered, "I bet you look awful!"

My mother shushed her. Then my dad chuckled, "Cassandra, how you get yourself in these pickles constantly is beyond me. You must get it from your mother's side." A soft oof from him told me my mother had most likely elbowed him.

"Whatever you need us to do, Cassandra," my mother's soft voice replied. "Tell me what you're seeing."

"We have a pentagram in a cemetery to start," I stated.

"Oh, they weren't playing, were they?" my dad asked.

My mom's soft voice changed in an instant to commanding. "We're first going to return energy. I need everyone to turn on their speakerphones." Her voice echoed around us as we all complied with her instructions. "Next, everyone stand on a point of the star. Cass, put your phone on one of the points. You have another job to do."

Someone had cleared the circle of any debris, and it was fully intact again. Bear moved Zander out of the circle and leaned him against a nearby headstone. One by one, Alice, Bear, Piper, and Hazel each chose a point to stand on. Quickly, I placed my phone on the empty point and backed away.

In the center, Dolores was starting to move again, but her eyes remained closed. Outside of the circle, I stood and listened to the instructions from my mother.

"Everyone, place your phones at your feet then raise your hands to shoulder height with palms facing outward," she commanded, her voice repeated around the circle. She was in surround sound and her voice echoed in the vast cemetery.

They each followed her instructions.

"Now, Cassandra, plant your feet and I want you to draw in energy to you with your hands."

My arms and hands made small circles, moving out, up, and down in front of me. "Make sure you take slow breaths and concentrate on gathering that energy," she added.

With a slow, even breath, I shut my eyes and focused on the energy around me.

My mom said, "Do not leave your spots, that is essential. No matter what happens. We cannot break the formation. Now, repeat after me." She began a soft chant. "You will return what you have stolen."

Our group faithfully repeated my mom's words. The phones picked up our chant and doubled our words around the circle.

"Lifeforces wish to return to their proper places," she said and the circle repeated.

"I call upon the watch towers of the east, north, south, and west to watch over us," she said. We repeated.

"Whatever negative energy you have sent to Cassandra, we send back to you threefold."

I sensed a bright light and slowly opened my eyes and saw Dolores shining in silver. The silver thread floated in the air above her.

With even vigor in my hands, I pulled the air and tried to entice the thread to abandon Dolores. Inch by inch, it grew in length as it detached itself from her limp body. When it snagged under her, the force of the thread as it extracted itself rolled her body over.

It floated higher into the air and made a beeline for me. A glowing light from my chest pulsed while my own thread protruded from me. It began to extend forward until it was taut and reached out toward Dolores. Slowly, the threads lengthened until finally, the two reached the edge of the circle. Without touching, the threads drifted in the breeze. For a brief second, I feared that they would not meet.

Then electricity zapped through me and Dolores as the threads met and joined. As they fused together, Dolores seized on the ground. Despite the continued shocks and quivers that ran through my body, I grabbed hold of the thread. Gently, I pulled at it and hoped to further unwind it from Dolores. Energy began to seep into me from Dolores.

She shook her head and her eyes snapped open. With a howl, she sat up and yelled, "No," when she saw the thread. Her hands grabbed it and pulled it back.

I held onto the thread tighter, and my fists began to ache. With a swift yank, Dolores pulled hard again and I felt the thread slip through my hands. Quickly, I wrapped the thread around the backs of both of my hands and dug my feet behind a nearby tombstone.

My mother's voice called out, "What you have stolen wishes to return to its rightful place. We release the energy you have taken against its will and return it to Cassandra." In a chant, we repeated the sentences over and over.

Slowly, the glow surrounding Dolores seemed to dim. First from her feet, where the thread had begun to unravel, then up her ankles, shins, and thighs. No matter how hard she gripped the thread, it slipped from her fingers as if she was putting forth no effort.

It unraveled from her torso and up to her neck and chin. When the final loop released itself from Dolores, she shrieked and fell back to the ground.

Her skin sagged and gave the impression that it had been stretched beyond its limits. She reminded me of what I imagined Baba Yaga would look like.

I looked at my hands and arms. The liver spots and wrinkles had disappeared. My fingers trailed over my face to find smooth skin. I was me again. "Mom, I've got it back!," I shouted.

My mom's voice called out, "Spirit that was brought here against nature, it is time for your return to the beyond. Begone from here and go back from whence you came and never shall you walk this earth. Begone and be forgotten."

From the center of the pentagram a red glowing hole appeared. Heat wisped up and warmed our faces.

Dolores scrambled to her feet, unsteady and wobbly. Her wild eyes were wide and bloodshot. Carefully, she took steps back from the hole until she was at the edge of the circle.

But when she tried to step over the circle, something prevented her escape. I suspected Bradley and Jason were there and blocked her.

Slowly, from the hole a jagged fissure appeared and zigzagged its way to Dolores' feet. When she tried to step over one of them, it widened. Shards of ground broke off and fell down into the deep abyss.

She was trapped.

From the fissure a deep, thick voice hissed, "There you are, Dolores. We've been scouring the underworld for you."

"No!" she cried, but a dark red clawed hand reached out

from the ground and wrapped its fingers around her ankle. Ineptly, she tried to kick at the hand, but she stumbled and fell hard onto the ground. Swiftly, the hand jerked on her ankle and began to drag her toward the hole.

Dolores turned over and dug her fingernails into the ground. The hand continued to drag her, and her fingers left long lines in the ground. As she reached the mouth of the hole, the hand tightened its grip on her and laughed. "It's time to come back home, Dolores. And this time, there will be no escaping."

In an instant, she was pulled down into the hole. Her screams slowly faded as she fell out of sight.

Only when the red glow had extinguished did any of us breathe a sigh of release.

Twenty

It's a New Day

We walked out of the cemetery as the sun began to rise. Work needed to be done to heal the land that had been so horribly desecrated.

We filled in the pentagram. Bear had gone to his house to grab a rake. We filled in the ruts and grooves with clumps of grass. We added dirt to areas to fill in spaces between the clumps, followed by dashes of holy water. Alice had run to our motel room and gathered the water and crystals. With incredible care, Alice placed the crystals around the area, in the hopes of protecting the land.

My mom further aided us, by guiding us through a healing meditation and blessing for the space. In her closing, she recited, "And may those with evil wills and hearts never be welcomed here now or ever."

By the time we were done, the area with the pentagram was barely noticeable. The fissure in the ground was beyond our abilities. It would be up to the authorities to decide what had happened and let the public know of their theory.

We would let Zander wake on his own. Conveniently, if he was found by the grounds keeper, the gun he had used to keep the police busy most of the night was set next to him.

Alice held Zander's phone in her hands. "He doesn't need this," she announced as she tossed his phone deep into the woods. The sound of it hitting a tree told us it was beyond repair.

As we neared the entrance of the cemetery, I could see hundreds of spirits lined up on the road. My legs wobbled again and Bear put my arm over his shoulder to steady me. The exhaustion hit me square in the chest and irritation sparked in my belly. I whispered, "I intend to go home. To sleep." No matter how hard I tried, the irritation snuck into my tone. "You're all free now. Return to your places."

Bradley whispered in my ear, "They can't. They're waiting for you to help them return to where they've come from. It's sometimes hard for us spirits to travel too far from our places. You are a beacon and have proven that you can transport us."

"The shimmer I exude, right?" I said with annoyance.

I opened my mouth to address the spirits, but Bradley spoke before I could., "Cassandra will help you. Jason and I will as well. But now, she needs rest. We will keep you updated as soon as she has restored her full strength."

The spirits vanished, but I could sense their presence. They followed behind us.

Without warning, Bear swooped me up into his arms. Instantly, my heart fluttered. *So that's what that feels like!* I had never been swept off my feet before.

"Bear, thank you, but I can walk," I said wearily. "It's too far to carry me."

"Shh. I've got you," he whispered.

Instantly, a future relationship requirement was unlocked. If I was ever going to fall in love, the person would need to physically be able to sweep me off my feet.

Once we were back to my motel room, Bear gently set me down, and my bed called to me. Alice, however, guided me to the bathroom and started the shower for me. Piper placed a pair of clean pajamas on the tank of the toilet while Hazel turned down the lights around the room.

Bear left us to go into the adjoining room and gave us some privacy.

As soon as the water hit my skin, I felt tears slip down my cheeks. The energy drain, stress, and terror of the night hadn't allowed me to acknowledge any of my emotions. Now, with exhaustion and time, they all poured out of me until I was snot-faced and puffy-eyed. I deserved to cry, and I didn't care what I looked like.

I cried as I washed my hair and body. Long sobs escaped my chest as I let the water wash away the film on my skin. When the suds were cleared from my body and the tears had finally stopped, I shut the shower off. Grit from dirt and gravel slowly swirled down the drain.

On the back of the door hung a warm fuzzy robe that didn't belong to me. One of the women had gone to their house to let me borrow theirs. I slipped it on over my pajamas and made my way to the sink outside the bathroom.

Quickly, I brushed my teeth and made my way to the bed. Light cafe jazz, which was a favorite of mine, played softly from my cellphone. Someone had pulled the covers back for me.

I climbed into the bed and as soon as I shut my eyes, I felt my consciousness fall away and I slept.

No dreams plagued me, just blissful darkness.

Hours later, only when my stomach began to grumble, did I wake. Like returning from the dead, my eyes were crusted shut and I had to peel them open. Aches and pains radiated everywhere on my body.

At the table in the corner, Bear sat while he read a book with a booklight. He greeted me with a smile the moment he saw I was awake.

He shut off his booklight and placed a bookmark in his book. Then gently, he asked, "Hey, how are you doing?"

"Ok," I replied. A groan escaped me as I shifted to sit up. My shoulder joint protested my movement. "I'm hungry."

"I figured you'd be up soon. I had Piper and Hazel go out to grab lunch for everyone," he said and checked the time on his phone. "They should be back any minute."

"What book are you reading?" I asked.

"Château Merlot. It's about vampires that keep people like wine cellars," he replied with a wink. Then he got up, walked to the adjoining room, and shut the door behind him.

While I waited, I carefully began to stretch my body. Toe curls, ankle flexes, and wrist circles. I took my time on each joint. Slowly, I was able to get up from bed. Someone had set out a pair of clothes for me on the counter. Throughout the night, my friends had taken care of me. I was sure that they had taken turns watching over me in all the ways that they could.

I carefully got dressed and leaned against the bed to change my underwear and pull my pants on. I didn't need to fall and not be able to get up. The image of being found half dressed with my butt hanging out of my pants brought redness to my cheeks. For good measure, I pulled my hair up into a ponytail.

From next door, I could hear voices as the door opened and shut. It sounded like Hazel and Piper were back. Moments later, the adjoining room door opened slowly, and Alice's voice called, "Are we ready for lunch?"

I walked to her and opened the door the rest of the way. "Yes, I am," I replied and pulled her into a tight hug.

The group came over and placed bags of food onto the small round table. Each of us was given a box with our lunch inside. Whatever they ordered smelled heavenly. The joy I felt when I opened my box and found a perfectly golden grilled cheese resting on a bed of French fries, sans pickle cannot be understated.

There is nothing more healing than a grilled cheese sandwich. I wished I could have savored the sandwich, but my hunger drove me to eat faster and within moments, it was devoured. The only thing better would have been a milkshake to dunk the fries in.

The sentiment was mimicked around me as each of my friends ate like they hadn't in a year either.

Alice and Bear gathered everyone's empty boxes when we were done and took them to the trash can.

Bradley's gentle grumble let me know he was present. "When you're ready, there are a lot of spirits that could use your help to get home. But first, I think you need to clean up in there. Jason and I can't get in with all that salt."

Without a word, Hazel made a slash mark in the line and dashed to the main office. Moments later, she ran back with a vacuum and sucked up the salt. A sigh of relief escaped me as I felt the last dredges of fear disappeared. Dolores and Doyle were gone.

I became overwhelmed with the task of returning so many ghosts. My mind instantly began imagining how many locations the spirits would need to be taken to. The way I thought about it made my brain hurt and seemed too complicated and added to my feelings of being overwhelmed.

"Any suggestions on how to do this?" I asked the group.

Jason replied, "You don't need to worry about that. Bradley and I have them sorted by distance."

Tears pricked my eyes. Even my ghost friends had taken care of me. "Thank you."

"You would have made it into a whole production. They'd want you to hear each one of their stories and you would have indulged them. They're a chatty group and if I know anything about chatty people, when they get together, there's no easy way to make them shut up again. I'm saving myself time and boredom here," Bradley said, but without his usual gruffness to his voice. "They're impatient, but what's a few more hours going to matter to them?"

"How do I return them?" I asked. "I've never transported so many before."

Bear asked, "Could you rent a bus? Or a U-haul?"

"If we get them close enough to Cassandra, they'll most likely...stick," Bradley said.

"Like gum on a shoe?" Piper asked disgustedly.

"Essentially," Bradley replied. "They are determined to get back to where they belong, so they'll do whatever it takes to return. If that means that they float alongside the car as you drive, then so be it. It's not like they can die again. No matter how terrible of a driver someone is."

"I'm not a bad driver," I replied.

"I never said that about your driving, but perhaps the old saying about people who protest too much is true," he added.

"Anyways, let's get this show on the ghost bus," Jason rushed.

With a nod, I led the group outside. Most of the spirits were invisible, but I could hear their nervous chatter. I could only imagine how difficult it was to be away from a place that you were attached to.

For the first time in too long, I felt a pull to return home. Mom and Dad were of course my comfort providers, but the desire to see my sisters was overwhelming. It had been a while since I had seen them.

With no other person in our group with the ability to speak to spirits, they pressed closer to me and sought my attention.

Alice stood on the side and took photos. The disappointed scowl on her face told me she didn't capture anything. Bear, who moved to stand next to her, took a photo with his phone. His eyes widened and slowly he turned his phone to show Alice. She groaned softly and asked, "How did you get a photo and I didn't?"

Bear shrugged and Alice continued to take photos.

Despite the fact that the spirits had already been sorted, they pressed in on me, and I felt suffocated by the sheer number of spirits around me.

"Can you back up, please?" I asked, but they didn't seem to hear me. Again, I asked, "Can you back up?" Still, they didn't listen.

Bradley's gruff voice yelled, "Everybody move!" Almost instantly, they followed his instructions. "I've always wanted to say that." He chuckled.

Collectively, I felt the spirits take a step back. While they had overwhelmed me, it was phenomenal to sense a release from the effects Doyle had put onto them. Their fear had dissipated and they were ready to go home.

"Ok, Bradley and Jason, we're going to start with the spirits that belong in the cemetery," I said.

"Gotcha!" Jason replied. Then he called out, "Group One! You're up!"

"Which group is that?" I heard a few spirits say.

Bradley shouted, "It's the cemetery crew."

After a few moments, a neat row of spirits lined up in the parking lot. "Ok! We need Cecil H, Stephen M, Helen L, Dana G, and Larry P," Jason called out.

The five spirits gathered around me. "It's time to take you back. You all belong back at the cemetery," I said.

They all nodded. A tall woman raised her hand and said, "I'm Helen. I'm a little scared to go back into the cemetery." The rest of the spirits murmured their agreement.

"That's understandable. I'm going to go back with you, and you'll see that the danger is gone. Plus, my mom added a little extra spice in there to make sure the place is safe in the future," I replied.

For the first time, I walked to the cemetery without anyone forcing me to go. No one was coercing me. No one was whisking me away in the night.

Alice, Bear, Piper, and Hazel followed behind me. The gravel crunched under our feet. We were all silent, which gave my mind a moment to form some questions. What had Doyle made me do the night I rescued Violet? The cuts on my feet were the only proof I had of my unintended trip.

I cleared my throat and asked the group, "Doyle manipulated me to go to the cemetery. I assume I walked inside, but I have no memory of that night after I went to bed."

"Larry here," one of the spirits said. "He used you to call the spirits from further away. Once they arrived, Doyle bound them to the cemetery. Luckily, he couldn't keep you for long."

Helen added, "Doyle had to sleep sometime. He wouldn't have been able to keep both the spirits and you under his spell when he was unconscious. So, once he was done with you, he guided you back to your motel room."

"I'm glad I can help everyone get back to their rightful places tonight to make up for my involvement in their imprisonment," I said.

"It wasn't your doing," Larry replied.

Before long, we stood outside of the cemetery. Across the entrance, yellow police tape barred people from entering.

Alice replied, "It's not a good idea for us to enter. We're lucky none of us were harmed, and we shouldn't press our luck further."

"I agree," I said. "Go be at peace, my friends. May the place you've been laid to rest remain safe and secure for you for the rest of eternity."

One by one, the spirits waved goodbye and disappeared into the cemetery.

Alice and I stood side by side for a few moments before she bumped her hip into mine. "Five down, only 245 more to go," she said. We linked arms and turned back to the motel only to find that the spirits had followed us.

The sky began to darken as the sun dipped closer to the horizon. Stars would begin to sparkle in the sky soon.

Jason, his outline softly glowing in the shadows of the trees, explained, "They wanted to witness to make sure you kept your word."

"So, we didn't need to do all that work of sorting them?" I

asked.

He shook his head. "Best laid plans, am I right?"

I shrugged. "Onto the next!," I roared. The spirits met my cry and Alice jumped.

With a shaky voice, Alice asked, "Did you hear that?"

A laugh boomed out of my chest as I said, "That was the sound of 245 ghosts ready to be returned to where they belong."

After two hours of returning spirits to the north of Wisconsin Dells, my stomach had begun to grumble. The locations that remained were south of the motel.

"Hey everyone!" Alice called out. "We're going to let Cassandra get some rest and food."

Bear nodded and led us back to the motel. The moment I saw my bed, the desire to get into it was too much to resist.

"I'll only lay down for a few moments," I lied as I crawled into bed.

Bear, Piper, and Hazel spoke quietly to Alice before they left.

Alice sat at the table and replied, "Get some sleep. The others are going to get us some dinner. I'll wake you when it's here."

In a moment I was asleep.

Twenty-One

Breakaway

What seemed like only a second, Alice gently patted me awake. "Cassandra, dinner is here," she cooed to me. "My mom also gave me a bag of cheeses for you to take with you."

With all the effort I could find, my eyes opened. Over me, Alice held a box that smelled delicious and my stomach growled in response, like it was a wild animal and starved.

I sat up slowly, forced myself not to snatch the box out of Alice's hands and tear into it. Instead, I thanked her and got out of bed. After I used the bathroom, I made my way to the table to sit with her.

I took a bite of my slice of lasagna. Tears sprang to my eyes as I was instantly reminded of my mom's recipe. It was about time I returned home. I needed my mom. I needed the safety of her arms. "Where are the others?" I asked.

Alice smiled and answered, "They had a few things to do.

Their parents are friends and they have an autumn cookout every year. Their presence was required."

"Why aren't you with Bear?" I asked, then shoved another bite into my mouth.

She blushed and shook her head. "We're not together, together. We haven't had a lot of time to define what we are. Plus, even if we are *together*, I don't know if we would be ready to announce it to our parents yet."

"That makes sense," I said. "Why would you not know, seeing as all the two of you do when you're in each other's presence is to look like you're lovelorn."

Alice opened her mouth but then closed it again.

I shook my head and said, "I don't have to be psychic to see what you both mean to each other. You'll figure this out soon. After I get these spirits back to where they belong, my time will be up here."

Tears pooled in her eyes. "But I'm not ready for you to leave," she cried.

Before I knew it, tears were spilling down my cheeks. "I know," I replied. At the same time, we got up and hugged each other.

"If only I could take you with me," I cried.

With the back of her hand, she wiped away her tears. "Currently, I'm without a job, so my calendar is open," she laughed.

"You're without a job," I repeated as if the information was brand new to me.

Confusion tinted her tone as she replied, "Yeah, you were there."

I was quiet for a long moment before I replied, "Have you ever thought about being a personal assistant? There's no one else I would trust more to have my location and my back."

"But I'd have to move, huh?" she asked.

"I don't believe so. My last PA lived in Detroit. Jack brought her on. I mean, there are times when she would travel to Emberford to help on set, but we don't film year-round. You could stay here, do the remote stuff and when it's time to shoot, travel to me for a few weeks. We could have sleepovers every night!" I said, hopeful.

With defeat in her tone, she replied, "But I've never done PA work before."

"What the hell do you call the last two weeks?" I raised my voice.

"It was closer to ten days," she mumbled.

I let my head drop back in exasperation and then said, "You arranged for me to meet your friends. Took me around to some of the best spots, and helped get me to and from everywhere. Hell, you helped send Dolores back to wherever she had come from. That was a whole lot of personal assistance."

Alice nodded hesitantly, almost as if she were still unsure of herself. "I've got a horrible job track. I break and drop things," she stated.

"Good news is that most of the time, you'll be remote. Retrieving jelly for me isn't a task that should be on your responsibility list. When we're together, you'll be more comfortable than you ever were at that grocery store, " I said, trying hard to convince her to take the job.

She played with her fingers and moved the toe of her shoe over the carpet. Finally, she answered, "Only if you *really* want me."

I pulled her into a hug again and we began jumping up and down together. "Yes!" I said.

When we finally stopped jumping and hugging, Alice asked me, "What about Bradley? What's he going to do?"

"I'm not sure. I'll have to have a conversation with him about that. Maybe he's where he wants to be, and he'll stay here. But I'll have to take Jason back with me so he can rest," I replied. "Would you like to go with me to return the other ghosts?"

She nodded and I grabbed a notepad that had locations in order of distance from the motel. Someone had written them down for me while I had slept. Alice grabbed our purses, keys, and cellphones, and we closed the door behind us.

"Hey Bradley?" I asked, unsure of where he had gone.

"Yeah?"

"Will my plan to get the spirits back work? Will they stick to the outside? Or do we make the world's largest clown car? Will they be able to all fit in? Or will they need to float beside us and try to keep up?" I asked.

"World's largest clown car?" he asked.

"You're the first spirit I transported long distances. I'm not sure how that works," I said.

Before he spoke, he exhaled a sigh of exasperation. "They'll either squeeze in or float beside the car. But I call shotgun."

As soon as we were in my car, I rolled down the window. With my head stuck out of the car, I called to the spirits, "We're hitting the road. If you don't want to be stuck here, you'd better come with me." The spirits followed us as we began to slowly drive down the street toward the downtown area.

As each spirits' location neared, they floated ahead of us and we followed down side streets and into neighborhoods.

An exhale of relief escaped every single spirit as they stood at the entrance of their space. A home, a cemetery, a river, a grove of trees, a park, a shop, and a church. We returned spirits to them all.

As we delivered the spirits, they turned back one final time to us and waved goodbye.

Finally, the crowd of spirits had dwindled, but those that remained didn't guide us anywhere. They followed us and whispered, "We're not close. Still so far away." It became crystal clear that the spirits left had destinations that were further away.

Bradley said, "It's going to be a long night."

Twenty-Two

We're Off To See The World

The rest of the night, Alice, Bradley, and I drove the group of ghosts back to their rightful places. I constantly caught sight of them outside the windows and in the mirrors. Luckily, it was late and traffic was almost non-existent. I could drive however slowly I needed without worry of irritating other drivers. We had followed the addresses listed in the notepad to drive to so we would be close for each spirit in tow.

With still around a hundred spirits to deliver, there weren't intimate send offs. As soon as a spirit got close enough to their destination, they released themselves from me and disappeared into the night. It felt like I was a spiritual papergirl, tossing spirits instead of papers to houses and businesses.

By the time the final three spirits shuffled off, Alice was asleep in the back seat.

We were miles outside of Wisconsin Dells and it would take

time for me to drive us back. When my eyes started to become heavy, I opened up my window and appreciated the chilly air that hit me in the face. Too soon, though, my eyes threatened to close again.

"Bradley?" I asked.

"Yeah?" he answered immediately.

"What are your plans now? Is there anywhere you need me to take you?" I asked.

He grumbled and made soft noises for a long time. Right about the time I had convinced myself that he was annoyed that I had asked him, he said, "Everything has been checked off of my Wisconsin Dells list, except for one thing."

"Oh, really? And what is that?" I inquired.

"I'd like to go to a supper club. My parents always made it a priority to go, but they would leave me with a local babysitter. I've never gotten to go to one," he replied softly.

"Any specific one in mind?" I asked.

"No, whichever one, you'd like to go to," he answered.

"You know you can't eat, right? Can't taste it," I replied.

"But I can remember," Bradley said softly.

I nodded and said, "When we get back, I'll check into it and see if we can squeeze it in before we go," I replied.

We were quiet for a while, but I still needed to know what his plans were after the supper club.

"What happens after the supper club? I'm going back to Emberford tomorrow. Where do you want to rest? I'm happy to take you wherever you want, within reason," I replied.

With surprise, he said, "Oh! That's thoughtful of you and all, but I'm not done with my bucket list yet."

"But what about the supper club? You said you had one last thing," I uttered.

"Yes. One last thing in the Dells. But my bucket list is far from being complete," he stated.

"Exactly how many *things* are on your bucket list?" I asked, afraid of the answer.

"Too many to count, I'm afraid. Luckily, it's mostly Midwest places. I'd like to touch all of the Great Lakes. But I wouldn't mind seeing the Grand Canyon, Atlantic and Pacific Oceans," he declared.

"And I'm sure all the places in Europe and the Caribbean too, huh?" I said stiffly.

"Ew. No. You have to get one of those passports and only stuck-up people get those. I'm not a bougie person," he replied.

"You know you don't need a passport anymore, right?" I stated.

He grumbled and then asked, "You want my bucket list to get bigger?"

"I don't know what you want me to do about this," I said. "What exactly do you want? Be specific because I'm still not sure what you're looking for."

He took a deep breath and answered, "Cassandra, would I be able to stay with you? Travel when we can to places on my bucket list. What use is it to have a last name of Seer and not be able to see the country we live in?"

"I have to work. You're not going to be paying for any of these trips," I said.

"You can't put a price on this kind of thing. You've already proven how frugal you can be. It's just…" he said and then trailed off.

"Hmm?" I asked.

"The spirits that were trapped in that cemetery were all anxious to return to their places. Almost like they felt an intense pull to be home. I don't get any such pull. The only pull I have is to be near you. Please let me come back with you," he replied.

How could I refuse? "Of course you can. But my family are all psychics as well. You have to be considerate to them all," I stated.

"Understood."

Bradley was now going to be my permanent hitch-hiking ghost, and I was his tour guide to help him on his quest to complete his bucket list.

As soon as we arrived back at the motel, I gently woke Alice up. We shuffled inside and she promptly fell back to sleep.

I sat at the table in the room and researched supper clubs while Bradley grumbled over my shoulder.

"None of the ones here in the Dells will open early enough. I'd like to head out shortly after checkout," I told him.

"Hmmm. That's understandable. What if… What if we found one on the way? It doesn't *have* to be one here, especially since my parents didn't take me. I don't even know which one they would go to," he compromised.

"Wow. That's extremely decent of you. I'm truly surprised," I remarked.

"Don't get used to it. I'm still a crotchety old man, but it's the least I can do," he replied.

With Bradley's input, we found a supper club in Lake Geneva that he wanted to see. I noted the name and address of the restaurant and yawned. Quickly, I got into pajamas and got ready for bed.

In the morning, I began to pack up my things. The check out time was at eleven am, and I needed to return home. I had to find a new agent and get Alice brought on as my personal assistant. Not to mention informing my parents that I had returned home with a new ghost for our house. I didn't think they would mind, but they were sometimes hard to read. Luckily, we had an attic and basement that he may like that weren't being used by anyone in the family, past or present. I could spruce up his space to make it more comfortable for him.

When I shut the motel door behind me, Alice, Bear, Piper, and Hazel stood in the parking lot in a line, waiting to tell me good-bye.

I hugged Alice quickly and whispered, "I'm so excited to work with you."

Bear was next. He hugged me close and I whispered in his ear, "Finalize what's going on with you two, ok? You're crazy about her, so be brave and let her know how you feel." He nodded and I moved onto Piper.

"Thank you for all your help with the events. You are spectacular at what you do," I said and pulled her in for a hug. "Maybe someday, we can work together again."

"I would *love* that," she replied and then pulled back from the hug. "Don't be a stranger, ok?"

I nodded and Hazel pulled me into a hug. "Take care of yourself, ok?" she whispered. "Just because you're heading back to Michigan doesn't mean you can get rid of us that easily. We're going to come visit you ASAP, ok? You can take us around the sites of your town."

A dry lump in my throat made it hard to talk so instead I laughed half-heartedly. "It'll take about twenty-two minutes to see all the sites."

I took my key back to the main office and thanked the owner for a wonderful stay.

"Thank you for staying, and I hope you'll come back again," he said.

I would stay again if I ever came back to the Dells.

Bradley, Jason, and I got into my car and waved goodbye to my new friends.

Jason's family lived in Fallasburg, Michigan, and we would cross the river that Jack had killed him at. It was a long journey ahead, but Jason deserved to be reunited with his family.

As I researched our choices of routes ahead, an alert on my phone chimed.

A bright red headline that announced there was breaking news:

Cassandra Seer, *The Emberford Psychic*, In Hot Water.

I had never opened an article so quickly. "What did I do now?" I screeched.

The article read:

Cassandra Seer, *The Emberford Psychic* (Now streaming on *Echo*), has a scandal before her new show has even been renewed for another season.

Ms. Seer lives in Emberford, Michigan and has found recent success as a reality TV psychic.

An Emberford resident, who requested not to be named for her protection, revealed that scandals are nothing unusual for the new celebrity or her family. "She attracts attention… demands it in fact. Ms. Seer is an abomination and a fraud. No one has the abilities she and her family claim to have."

Earlier this month, Cassandra Seer found herself topless at the beach and her blurred photos appeared on the cover of *Observer Weekly*.

Again, her name is on the lips of the media as her former agent, Jack Kress, has been arrested for the murder of Jason

Freedlander.

Jason Freedlander had gone missing five years ago. In a shocking confession at a viewing party for her show Cassandra Seer was holding while on vacation up in Wisconsin Dells, Jack confirmed what had happened to the young man.

Yesterday, a dive team ventured into the Grand River to search for the missing teen's vehicle. A positive ID on the car was made by the license plate still attached. Human remains were found inside the vehicle, but further identification is required.

Time will tell if this scandal will hinder or catapult Cassandra Seer's career, unless Ms. Seer has time to give us an insight into what's going to come.

"Gah!" I yelled. "That whole article is click bait! I had nothing to do with this. Jack was the one who killed you, Jason. Not me."

"Well, you know, there is no such thing as bad publicity," Jason said, attempting to comfort me.

Bradley added brightly, "At least you didn't end up accidentally naked on the cover of a tabloid again."

"You're both trolls, you know that?" I asked in exasperation.

They both snickered and howled with laughter.

"Whenever you're ready to hit the road, I'd appreciate not being laughed at while I drive," I snapped.

Twenty-Three

The Bottomless Pit

We drove for two hours to Lake Geneva, where the supper club was. Bradley had me painstakingly look at all the supper clubs south of The Dells, until he finally chose The Sidecar Supper Club. Lucky for us, it opened earlier on Wednesdays.

When I had perused the menu online and got over the initial shock of the menu prices, I planned what I was going to have ahead of time.

"I'm going to have some cheese curds and a drink," I announced to my ghosts.

"Generally, day drinking is set aside for those that are alcoholic or have had a rough bit of life. It's only 2 pm, remember?" Bradley asked. "I'd like to get back to Emberford with you. I've decided I don't much like hitchhiking."

Jason added, "Yeah. I don't know how comfortable I would be with someone who is intoxicated. Seeing as that's the reason

I'm dead."

I rolled my eyes. "I'm going to drink a soda."

The supper club was an old house converted to a restaurant with many additions built onto the building. Over the front door, a neon sign announcing cocktails and dinner shone. The Sidecar Supper Club's parking lot was partially filled with patrons.

After parking the car, I got out and walked to the building. I was greeted by a hostess.

"Welcome!. How many in your party?" she asked.

"Thr…I mean one," I said, forgetting no one could see or hear my ghosts who had followed me inside.

"Do you have a reservation?" she asked doubtfully.

"No. I'm on my way home, and someone mentioned how incredible supper clubs were and decided at the last minute to stop," I rambled.

"Oh. Well, we have a large party due any time," she replied as she checked the watch on her wrist. "I can put you on the waitlist, but I can't say how long you'll have to wait."

I nodded and then asked, "Would I be able to sit at the bar? I don't need a ton of attention."

The hostess' face lit up and she said, "Yes! That would be incredible!" Quickly, she picked up a menu and walked me toward the bar. She pointed at me and made eye contact with the bartender before she returned to her post.

I took a seat in a brown leather high backed bar stool and opened the menu. The short, young bartender walked over to me and he asked, "What can I get for you?" His name tag read Gerald. He had black hair and a tight smile.

"An order of cheese curds and whatever your cola is," I said and placed the menu down on the bar top.

"Great," he replied and entered my order into the tablet he held. Then he stared at me. "You seem familiar to me. Have you been here before?"

I shook my head. "Nope. First time here," I replied.

He shrugged and went to other customers.

Soon, he placed my curds and drink in front of me, and I munched happily. Jason and Bradley were silent, and I was blissfully on my own for a short while. I hadn't been alone in longer than I could remember and found the distant chatter of patrons in the restaurant pleasant and relaxing. The sound of silverware on plates and clinks of glasses was like white noise.

Perched on my chair, I closed my eyes and enjoyed the solitude. There was a calm that, despite being in a group of people, there were no demands on me. No one needed me. No one tried to start a conversation with me. The only person in my orbit was the bartender.

When he refilled my soda, he asked, "Is there anything else I can get for you? Supper? Dessert?"

"No, thank you. Just the check."

As he passed me the check presenter he snapped his fingers and said, "I know why you look familiar!"

My solitude and calm evaporated in an instant. It could only last so long. I shut my eyes, afraid that he was going to announce to the entire restaurant that *The Emberford Psychic* was eating in their establishment.

Then he exclaimed, "You remind me of my mom."

My mouth dropped open. The bartender was pushing twenty-two, max. I did some rough math in my head. If his mother had him when she was sixteen, she would be…38. Grown.

I was old enough to have a full adult child.

The moment he saw my face, his smile dropped and he said, "It's a compliment. Here. Look." From his pocket, he pulled out his phone. He slid between a few photos of a lovely woman. There were some similarities; our full figures, brown hair and eyes. "You give off a caring vibe. It's almost like you radiate with love, just like my mom."

I glanced back up at Gerard and replied, "Thank you. Your mom sounds like a lovely person, and I'm honored to remind you of her."

I slid my credit card inside the slot of the booklet and passed it to him. Quickly, he ran my card and handed it back with the receipt. Once I put the card away and added a tip to the receipt, I ran to the restroom before we hit the road again.

After almost ten full hours on the road, an hour in construction, several "mini bucket list locations", and rest stops for me, we finally found ourselves driving along Lake Michigan.

"We're almost there," Jason announced as he hung his face out of the window.

"Here's one of the lakes you have on your bucket list, Bradley," I said as we pulled over so he could touch the lake. It was dark and I stayed in the car. Jason fidgeted in the backseat, impatient at being so close to his home.

When Jason could stand it no longer, he leaned out of the car and yelled, "Hurry up, Bradley!

A few moments later, Bradley grumbled and we knew he had returned. "Thanks for your patience," he hissed.

"I haven't been home in over five years. Pardon me, if I'm impatient. I need to get home," Jason countered.

"Alright, children. Do I need to separate you?" I asked as I shifted the car into drive.

"Don't do that," Bradley snapped. "I'm older than you."

"And you always will be," I said with a smile. I pulled onto the highway, and we were on the road again.

Jason began giving out directions, and I followed them instead of taking my GPS' advice. We drove around cities and through towns. He gave us stories, memories, and anecdotes while we drove, so it almost felt like he was our own tour guide.

"That house right there," he said as he pointed to a house that was an odd shade of pea green. "My mom grew up there and my dad lived right next door. They were only kids when they fell in love."

I slowed my speed so I could hear more of the stories that Jason shared, until finally, we arrived in Fallasburg.

His stories stopped abruptly and his directions became shorter. "Turn here. Go straight. Right. Left. Stop."

My GPS announced we had arrived on 11th Ave. The small white house was neat with light blue shutters on each of the windows. Lights shone through the windows and shadows moved as people walked by.

"This is my house," he said. "I need to go. I need to see them now. Thank you for everything."

Swiftly, he flew from the car and floated to the house. He stood outside on the small cement porch and gazed in through the large glass window in the front door. He took a step forward and then he was gone.

We sat in silence and watched the last place Jason had been, as if we expected him to say an official goodbye.

But he never came back.

I nodded after five minutes and pulled away from the house.

Bradley stayed quiet as we got onto the highway and headed for Emberford. It would take us a little under two hours to get there.

"So, I haven't sufficiently annoyed you," I said in an attempt to break the silence.

"I like to say that I haven't annoyed you sufficiently. You left me in that cemetery for almost a week," he replied with a sniff. "You deserve more payback, in my humble opinion."

"It was not almost a week. Three days, max," I replied.

"Seeing how I was kidnapped," he said.

"Ghostnapped," I interrupted.

"Ghostnapped," he repeated with a heavy sigh.

Silence spread between us as I realized that he could have been stuck in that cemetery for the rest of eternity.

I searched for words to begin the conversation with him, but I failed miserably and was left overwhelmed.

"It wasn't your fault," Bradley said suddenly. "Me being ghostnapped. While it took you longer than I would have liked, I had no doubt you were going to find me."

I nodded and felt a lump in my throat grow.

"It was quite surprising, however, when I discovered you had found a replacement ghost while I was gone. They can't be faulted for that. You do attract attention to yourself."

"You know I wasn't looking for you when I stopped in Beloit, right? I wanted to get away from ghosts. So, Jason wasn't a replacement. He was an addition," I said with a choked laugh. "I'm afraid to ask, but what did Doyle do to you?"

With a heavy sigh, he replied, "He caught me when I was out seeing the sights with that blasted flute of his. There was nothing I could do to resist it." He paused for a few beats before he continued softer. "Time there was even stranger than being dead. It was like a never-ending dream where everything was hazy and my thoughts were foggy. I wandered incessantly."

"While I'm glad that Doyle didn't torture you, that sounds

like a nightmare," I replied.

"If I had been more aware of what was happening, I think it would have felt the same way. It's only now that I'm out, the reality of the situation is setting in."

I nodded and drove in silence as my words evaporated before I could form them.

"The moment you stepped into that cemetery, the entire feeling shifted. There was a bright light that I instantly recognized as yours." He sighed softly and added, "Then I heard you jibber-jabbering and knew you had finally decided to come find me."

"Jibber-jabber? Really?" I asked.

"Yes. You never stop talking," he replied quickly. "Despite that, I've made a decision about my future."

"Oh, yeah? Do tell."

Quietly, Bradley answered. "I'm not ready to leave this world yet. Perhaps not ready to leave you yet. And I know you could use some guidance. Think of it as a service I'm offering you."

A laugh exploded out of me and I said, "You like me more than you thought you would."

His signature grumble answered me instead of an actual reply.

"I'll take that as a yes. I think you'll like my town. Everyone is super judgey. You'll fit right in," I replied with a smirk.

"Are there any resident lady ghosts that are single," he asked softly.

"I'm sure there are. We'll be close to the cemetery in town where you can go prowling for the ladies," I informed him. "Do ghosts date?"

Bradley sighed and asked, "Why not? If we're stuck here, why can't we have fun too?"

I nodded and replied, "True. I could be your matchmaker."

"That's a terrible idea. You're single. What on earth would you know about relationships?"

A disgusted sound escaped me. "Maybe I'll put you in the basement. I *was* going to offer you the attic, but now I'm not so sure."

"Thankfully, staying with your family means I'll have someone besides you to talk to. I wonder if they'll radiate light too?" he asked.

"I'm not going to put anything cozy in your area. I was going to offer you curtains, rugs, and knickknacks to make your space cozier. I don't think I care now," I replied.

"Again, I'm a ghost. In reality, I don't need that stuff anyways," he said and then added wistfully, "I mean, a pretty painting of a forest would be nice."

With a nod, I replied softly, "I've always wanted a house ghost. Here's hoping that we don't torture each other."

"If we do, I can always find somewhere else to go," Bradley replied.

"Maybe you'll finally share more about you. Tell me about family, friends, jobs, where you lived," I said hopefully.

"I'm not ready yet," he declined simply.

With a heavy sigh, I nodded. "That tracks for you."

I became thoughtful as the road lay ahead of us. My to-do list was steadily growing, but there was a sense of calm that ran through my whole body. For the first time since I had run away, I felt like myself again.

Better than myself.

And I suspected Bradley, too, felt something similar in himself. He was still invisible to me, but every once in a while I could see a light in the corner of my eye. We weren't best friends, maybe not even friends, but we were more than acquaintances. And if we could accomplish that, the sky was the limit.

There would be no more running. And I thought I had the best idea to claim my identity.

No sooner had we arrived at my house than I grabbed large pieces of paper and markers. Quickly, I began creating something that would stand out.

When the words were neatly printed on nine pieces of paper and taped together, I stapled them to thick pieces of cardboard. Then they were wrapped in clear packing tape. It wouldn't keep forever outside, but it would do until I could invest in something permanent. Finally, I attached some dowel rods and gently hammered them into the ground.

The sign faced my neighbors' house. She would no longer have power over me. I pulled up a chair on the front porch and waited for Mrs. Koch to make her appearance.

From where I sat, I could see her shadow move through the house and turning on lights. She moved from room to room, starting in the kitchen and making her way to the front door. She would need to get her slippers on to go outside to get her newspaper.

Squeak! Her front door opened and was quickly followed by a sharp WHACK of her screen door as it slammed shut.

Quickly, I stood up and corrected my posture. With my phone in hand, I pressed record, and a wide smile spread across my face. I wanted to be able to re-experience her response to my sign as many times as I needed.

Mrs. Koch slowly stepped down each step , but her eyes were fixed onto my sign. Her mouth moved as she read the words under her breath. Her face screwed up into a scowl which made her already wrinkly skin double or even triple over itself.

Then she read the sign out loud in her crackly voice, "*The Emberford Psychic* Lives Here! Have the afterlife you deserve." She spat on the ground in front of her and yelled, "You're going to hell."

"Nah. Sorry to break it to you, but I don't think so. They weren't interested in me," I laughed. "They're always searching for truly evil people." With one finger, I slowly pointed my finger at her. "You're unpleasant. I'd be careful if I were you. Just a F.Y.I., I brought home a new ghost. He's sticking around for a while. Don't irritate him too much. He's grumpy and he likes to travel." I paused and then added, "I bet the two of you will hit it off!"

When the record button was shut off, I waved my fingers at her and skipped into the house. I realized that everything that had happened over the past few weeks, or even months, wouldn't have happened if I had kept my abilities to myself. The good and the bad. The magazine cover, the friendships, Bradley, the ghosts that were captured and released, the confidence I had gained.

I was proud to be *The Emberford Psychic,* and no one was going to take that away from me.

Twenty-Four

Chapter Easter Eggs

Chapter 1 - The Fool - The cover is the imagining of the Fool Tarot Card with Cassandra

Chapter 2 - One in a Million - Bradley is called Bratley. One in a million is from the movie Miss Congeniality with Benjamin Bratt.

Chapter 3 - The Peanut Butter Solution - Reference is a 1980's movie about peanut butter. I still remember the nightmares I had after I watched this movie. This chapter deals with Cassandra purchasing peanut butter and jelly.

Chapter 4 - Extensive Collection of Name Tags & Hair Nets - Reference to the movie Wayne's World where Wayne shows off his collection of name tags and hair nets. This chapter Alice finds out she lost her job and will be adding to her name tag collection.

Chapter 5 - Lost in the Fog - Reference to The Others when Grace is lost in the fog looking for her husband. This is the name of the song that plays during that scene.

Chapter 6 - Annie & Molly - Reference from the movie Annie. Annie and Molly are best friends and they're always there for each other. Seemed fitting since Alice and Cassandra become fast friends.

Chapter 7 - Heart & Souls - This is a 1990's movie that I watched a ton as a teen. Cassandra listens to her instincts and goes into the woods to find the little girl.

Chapter 8 - Here Before- Barenaked Ladies song - This is probably my favorite band. This chapter has Cassandra going back to the cemetery against her will.

Chapter 9 - Kodo & Podo - Thieving ferrets in the 1980's movie, Beastmaster. Cassandra and Alice not only steal holy water from a church, but also nab salt from various places.

Chapter 10 - Dear Johnny - Reference from the movie Now & Then. Dear Johnny is the spirit that girls try to contact through a Ouija board in the cemetery. This chapter is the slumber party with a Ouija board.

Chapter 11 - King of Wishful Thinking - This is a reference to the song that plays in the 1990's movie, Pretty Woman, during Vivian's shopping scene. The girls in this chapter make

Cassandra go shopping.

Chapter 12 - Aces & Eights - This is a reference to a tavern in the 1980's Sierra video game, Quest for Glory I. This chapter is at the start of Cassandra's bar crawl for her TV show promotion her friends put together.

Chapter 13 - That's All I've Got To Say - This is reference to a song in Last Unicorn. This chapter we can only imagine what Alice and Bear have to talk about. I believe Bear and Alice talked...between make out sessions.

Chapter 14 - All Hell Breaks Loose - This is a reference to Supernatural season 2 episode 21 - Both this episode and the chapter have to deal with salt lines being broken.

Chapter 15 - Dangerous Type - Reference to the movie 1990's movie, The Craft. This is a song from that movie. I watched this movie so many times. This chapter deals with good vs evil and some truly dangerous type people.

Chapter 16 - Only the Lonely - Reference to the song by Roy Orbison. This is a CD that I took from my parents collection. They didn't seem to mind. At the end of this chapter, Cassandra watches Bear and Alice be able to escape from the cemetery, leaving her behind

Chapter 17 - Pit of Despair - Any Princess Bride fan will know this. If you haven't watched Princess Bride, I highly recommend. Cassandra is alone against Dolores.

Chapter 18 - As the World Falls Down - Reference to the 1980's movie, Labyrinth. Jim Henson shaped my childhood. It would be a crime not to acknowledge him somewhere in this list.

Chapter 19 - Relax. It's Only Magic - Here's another The Craft reference. This is the tagline to the movie. In this chapter, the group gets to practice a little magic, with the help of Cassandra's family.

Chapter 20 - It's a new Day - This is a reference to a song from the English dubbed version of Sailor Moon, released in the 1990's. This is the chapter that the group finally leaves the cemetery.

Chapter 21 - Breakaway - Reference to the Princess Diaries 2: Royal Engagement. Cassandra knows it's time to go home.

Chapter 22 - We're Off To see The World - This is a reference to the 1980's movie, The Chipmunk Adventure. This is one of the songs they sing as they head off on their adventure. Cassandra, Bradley, and Alice return the rest of the spirits to places that are further away from the Dells.

Chapter 23 - The Bottomless Pit - Reference to the 2000's movie, Spirited Away. This is a song that plays when No Face becomes a bottomless pit. This is the chapter that Cassandra and Bradley go to a supper club.

About the Author

Kari Pohar is a paranormal fiction author who grew up on her family's ghost stories and later decided to live out her destiny by moving into a house with occasional ghost visitors of her own. While mostly harmless, these spirits crossed a line when they started hanging around her children as infants—an experience that still haunts her today.

She's been married for twenty years, which suggests a surprising level of stability for someone so preoccupied with ghosts, vampires, and the undead. She submitted her first short story for publication on the morning her mother died, a fun fact that is not fun at all but does explain her fondness for dark humor and the paranormal. She draws inspiration from Edgar Allan Poe and O. Henry (minus the marrying-a-cousin part).

She has nine published short stories in a variety of anthologies and is the author of the vampire novel *Chateau Merlot*.

You can connect with me on:

- https://wilsonlindbergbooks.com/kari-pohar
- https://www.tiktok.com/@karipohar

Also by Kari Pohar

Château Merlot is a vampire owned apartment building where she houses her humans like a wine cellar

Château Merlot

Stephen was unaware of how valuable his blood was until Angelica Asta offered him a small fortune. In exchange, he must allow her to feed on him and live in the luxurious apartment complex, the Château Merlot. There, he discovers that there are some things that money can't buy.

When he attracts the attention of a brutal and conniving vampire, Stephen is forced to decide what his blood and life is worth. And time is running out.

Because they are thirsty.

www.ingramcontent.com/pod-product-compliance
Lightning Source LLC
LaVergne TN
LVHW010651110826
845149LV00014B/3033

* 9 7 9 8 9 8 9 9 4 6 9 6 9 *